ENTANGLEMENT

THE BELT: BOOK ONE

GERALD M. KILBY

Published by GMK, 2018
Copyright © 2018 by Gerald M. Kilby All rights reserved.
No part of this book may be reproduced, scanned, or distributed in any printed, or electronic form without express written permission.
Please do not participate in, or encourage piracy of copyrighted materials in violation of the author's rights. Purchase only authorized editions. This is a work of fiction. Names, characters, and incidents are either the product of the author's imagination or are used fictitiously. Any resemblance to actual persons, living or dead, businesses, companies or events is entirely coincidental.

Version 1.3

For notifications on promotions and updates for upcoming books, please join my Readers Group at www.geraldmkilby.com.

You will also find a link to download my techno-thriller REACTION and the follow-up novella EXTRACTION for FREE.

CONTENTS

1. Antiope Nine Zero	1
2. Hermes	6
3. Aria	16
4. Salvage	21
5. Rendezvous	28
6. Solomon	39
7. Cat And Mouse	46
8. Hidden Depths	57
9. Neo City Asteroid	73
10. Einstein, Podolsky, Rosen	88
11. Xiang Zu	101
12. Flight To The Docks	113
13. Purge	130
14. Weapons Check	134
15. The Gathering Armada	144
16. Twenty-One Days To Europa	153
17. Protocol Violation	163
18. Phone A Friend	170
19. Europa	173
20. Superluminal	189
21. Conclave	194
22. Change of Plan	204
23. Dyrell	213
24. Debris Field	220
25. Return to the Stars	236
26. Solomon's Dream	248
Also by Gerald M. Kilby	253
About the Author	255

1
ANTIOPE NINE ZERO

"Wake up, Commander. We have a situation."

Somewhere in the inner recesses of Commander Scott McNabb's slumbering subconscious, a series of synapses fired to alert his higher mind to incoming data. A voice... calling to him... one he knew... then it clicked. It was the ship's AI, Aria.

"Go away," was the most Scott was willing to utter by way of a reply.

"I'm sorry to wake you, Commander, but we have a situation that requires your attention."

Scott gave a low groan. "Is the ship compromised?"

"No, nothing that serious. The ship is fine. But..."

"Are we in any danger?"

"No, Commander. No danger. However..."

"Well then, just go away and let me get back to sleep." Scott buried his head further into the pillow.

"Commander, if I may..."

"Oh, for God's sake, Aria. You're the brains around here, you run the ship, what do you need me for?" There was a momentary pause, and Scott thought he heard the AI give an exasperated sigh, which was ridiculous; he must be dreaming it.

"I appreciate your confidence in my abilities. But a situation has arisen where protocol requires me to alert the ship's commander—that would be you."

It was Scott's turn to sigh. Aria would not leave him be until it said whatever had it all up in a heap. He excavated a hand from under the bedclothes and rubbed his face. "Okay, what is it?"

"My sensors have detected another ship close to the binary asteroid Antiope Nine Zero."

Scott scratched his head. "Another ship... this far out in the Belt?"

"Yes, Commander."

"Granted, that's unusual, Aria. But what? Is it alien or something?"

"Don't be ridiculous, Commander. The probability of an alien civilization existing that is capable of..."

"Okay, Aria... whatever." Scott waved a dismissive hand in the air. "So, what's the big deal?"

"It is a derelict spaceship, sir."

Scott raised his head from the pillow. "Derelict?"

"Yes, Commander. Derelict."

"As in dead?"

"Technically, a spaceship is not alive to begin with. But yes, there's no power signature and no signs of life. I have also tried to hail it several times. My initial analysis indicates it has been dead, as you put it, for several Earth years."

By now, Scott had rolled himself over face up on the bed. "I see."

"Protocol dictates that I must alert the commander in such a situation. We are required by the Outer Space Treaty to offer assistance to any vessel in difficulty. However, if we are to rendezvous with it, we must start deceleration as soon as possible. But you will need to give that order, Commander."

Scott sat up and scratched his chin, thinking. "So, if the ship is derelict, there would be salvage rights on it?"

"Assuming that everyone on the ship is dead, then yes."

Scott was beginning to realize that this just might be his lucky day. If they could claim salvage on this derelict ship, then the money would go a long way to solving a lot of Scott's problems—if not all of them. He stretched his arms and rubbed his face. "How long before rendezvous?"

"Approximately four hours."

"And deceleration?"

"We will need a seventy-two-minute burn."

"The crew are not going to like that, Aria."

"Indeed. However, the decision is yours and yours alone, Commander."

"Okay, Aria. Alert the rest of the crew. Tell them to strap in and prepare for deceleration. We'll meet up on the bridge after the burn. In the meantime, find out as much as you can about that vessel, particularly, eh... how much it might be worth in salvage."

"Will do, Commander. But I have found scant information on it so far."

Scott was now strapping himself into a seat in his cabin designed to mitigate the effects of the heavy gee experienced by deceleration. "That seems a bit strange. There must be some record of a vessel going missing out here."

"There is, but it's classified."

Scott's eyes widened. "Classified?"

"Yes, Commander."

Two thoughts now ran through Scott's mind in tandem. One, classified usually implied a whole pile of trouble, at best. At worst, it could be downright dangerous. There might be a damn good reason why this ship was lost, and that meant the crew of the Hermes could be exposing themselves to a potentially hazardous situation. The second thought he had, however, was more interesting: if this derelict craft was indeed part of a classified mission, the bonus for salvage just shot through the roof. Scott snapped on the last of the harness. "Have the others been alerted, Aria?"

"Yes, Commander. They're all strapped in now."

"Okay. Punch it." Scott felt the ship's powerful engines

kick in and he was slammed back into the seat. They would all be taking heavy gee for the next 72 minutes. Not pleasant, but it did give his mind a lot of time to consider how he was going to spend the salvage money—very pleasant indeed.

2

HERMES

By the time Scott arrived on the bridge of the Hermes, flight officer Miranda Lee was already there, standing beside the holo-table examining a gently rotating 3D display of the derelict vessel. She noticed him as he entered and looked up. "Well, if it isn't the commander of our great and glorious ship. Nice to see you on the bridge—for once."

Scott, having spent the best part of three years cooped up with this crew, had learned to ignore such jibes. But Miranda persisted, raising an arm to her chin in a mock pose of concentration. "Let me see, oh... it must be at least six months, maybe even nine?"

Again, he let it go. There was nothing to be gained by taking her on, as she could be quite intimidating when she wanted. Starting a row with her now would serve no useful purpose; it would only upset the delicate harmony that had been carved out by five people living in close proximity, far from civilization—and there were another two years to go. Instead, he smiled. "That's what happens when an AI runs the show: we all get made redundant."

"To be precise, Commander, I am a quantum intelligence—a QI, not an AI," Aria's voice resonated around the bridge.

"Yeah, whatever," said Scott, waving a hand in the air. He then nodded at the 3D rendering of the spacecraft hovering above the holo-table. "So, what do you make of it?"

Miranda leaned in on the table's edge. "Standard Excelsior class interplanetary transport. No torus, so no artificial gravity." She pointed to the back of the spaceship. "Looks like it had an engine upgrade to give it more thrust. It's also sustained a lot of damage just forward of the engine bay. See here." She paused the rotation of the 3D image and motioned at a spot toward the center of the vessel. But before Scott could take a closer look, both Cyrus Sanato, the ship's engineer, and Dr. Steph Rayman, the mission's medical doctor, came onto the bridge. Scott nodded a collective greeting and waved them over to the table. "Come—check this out."

"Jeez, what are the odds of finding something like this out here?" said Cyrus, moving in closer to the holo-table.

"Approximately, one point three billion to one," replied the disembodied voice of Aria.

Strictly speaking, Cyrus wasn't looking at the image of the spacecraft in the general sense of the word. That's because the ship's engineer had lost his sight in an accident when he was just a child. But that wasn't to say he couldn't see—far from it—as he was surgically fitted with enhanced biotech that enabled Cyrus to see the world in exquisite detail. Not only that, he could visualize in spectra far beyond the capabilities of the average human eye, those of infrared and ultraviolet, and in resolutions from the micro to the macroscopic. However, this hyper-vision required him to wear a wraparound visor permanently attached to his skull, the lenses of which were a dark reflective orange polished up to a high mirror finish. This, coupled with his bald head and squat physique, gave him the appearance of a bug and could be a little disconcerting on first encounter. Nevertheless, he had a permanent happy smile, bordering on a chuckle, and a disarming charm that made people warm to him instantly, regardless of his odd demeanor.

"Is this the best detail we've got on the craft, Aria?" Cyrus seemed to be adjusting something on the side of his head as he talked.

"We are still over two hours before rendezvous. The image will resolve better as we get closer."

"It makes a change from looking at rocks all the time," said Steph, who stood close to Cyrus at the holo-table.

Considering that their mission was to do a geotechnical analysis of the central asteroid belt, they spent a lot of time looking at rocks, as Steph put it. Yet that was the job. Yes, it could be monotonous, even downright boring, but that's what they all signed up for —except, perhaps, for Scott McNabb.

For him, the offer to command this mission had been a no-brainer. The way he saw it, the job gave him the money to clear some of his family debts. He could also get as far away as possible from certain individuals who were prone to visiting in the middle of the night—along with a few friends. They were the sort that had no problem explaining Scott's fiscal obligations through the subtle employment of a few well-placed kicks to the head.

As for the others, Scott didn't really know what their motivation was, nor did he care. You would think that after three years together they would know everything there was to know about each other, right down to their most intimate personal grooming habits. But, as a credit to the consortium that designed this mission, they were acutely aware that sticking five people together in a tin can for five years could be a recipe for disaster. It was entirely possible that one or more would go insane, or worse, become raging psychopaths. So, to protect their investment, they provided the mission crew with an exceptionally roomy—albeit very old—space station.

In many respects, it was overkill. The station was originally built to accommodate around a hundred and fifty people and had an enormous rotating torus that facilitated a very comfortable one-gravity environment. So, the five crew of the Hermes Asteroid Survey Mission could spread themselves out and, if they so desired, never actually meet another member of the team for weeks—if not months—on end.

The downside was that the ship was ancient. Some parts were estimated to be over ninety years old. It was virtually an antique. However, it had been retrofitted with new engines and a new reactor, although it still retained its original AI, Aria. This artificial intelligence had a quantum core, one of only a few in the solar system. As a result, it was far more capable than a standard AI and could run the entire ship—along with a good deal of the five-year mission—all by itself if it had to. In reality, Aria managed most of the actual survey by utilizing a wide range of spectral analysis systems. But every now and again, when an asteroid was deemed to be of significant interest, a more detailed survey would be required. This meant boots on the ground or, in other words, humans.

In these instances, a few of the crew would take one of the two small transport craft they had on board and physically land on the asteroid where they would mine for samples. Scott always looked forward to these mini-missions. It was a way of breaking the sheer, mind-numbing monotony of his existence. It was also a rare moment when they all came together and acted as a cohesive unit.

This felt like one of those times. So, with the crew now standing around a holo-table exchanging excited chatter, Scott was anxious to get the show on the road. "Aria, can you give us a summary of what we know so far?"

But before the QI had a chance to reply, Miranda broke in. "Shouldn't we wait for Rick to get here first?"

"Eh... yeah, of course. Aria, where is he?"

"Here."

Scott turned to see Rick Marantz striding onto the bridge, a mug of coffee in one hand and a taco in the other.

"Rick, you know you can't bring food onto the bridge."

"It's okay, buddy—I'll be careful," he said as a dollop of salsa snaked down his fingers.

Scott sighed. What was the point of even trying to maintain some sense of authority? No one seemed to care. "Okay, sure."

Rick was an old-school asteroid miner, and being sixty-three years old, was by far the oldest member of the crew. Some said he knew more about asteroids than even God did. He was easygoing, affable, and a man of few words. But swimming underneath the surface, Scott sensed deep emotional scars. Perhaps that's why they both had an affinity for each other. Two wounded souls just trying to survive.

"Okay, Aria, you can give us that summary now?" Scott quickly turned to Miranda. "If that's okay with you?"

The flight officer replied with a limp shrug.

"Can you two cut it out? I for one am sick to the back teeth of your constant bickering. Just do us all a favor and grow up." Everyone stopped and looked over at Steph. It was the standard reaction when she spoke, mainly because she seldom spoke. So, when she did, it was for a good reason and everybody had better pay attention. Scott wondered what it was about her that gave her such... authority, because he sure as hell didn't seem to have any. As far as Scott was concerned, when he spoke, nobody listened. So, like a pair of chastened school kids, Scott and Miranda called a truce as the QI began its summary.

"From what I can gather with the limited data available to me, the ship is an Excelsior class interplanetary transport vessel. Long-range scans indicate no power signature, no heat or radiation—in essence, no life whatsoever. The identity of the ship is still unknown. However, it closely matches the specifications of an Earth vessel that went missing somewhere in the asteroid belt while en route to the research colony on Europa, approximately three and a half Earth years ago."

At the mention of the words "Earth ship," Scott realized that they could be in for one hell of a payday.

The QI continued. "The ship has suffered severe impact damage just forward of the engines. Since this is the location of the main reactor, we can assume it was what proved to be fatal. I have also taken the liberty of informing central mission command on Ceres of the discovery and requested assistance in identifying the vessel."

"How long before we get a reply?" said Scott.

"This far out in the Belt, it takes approximately forty-six minutes for a message to be received. Therefore, I would estimate the minimum would be two hours, including the time taken to formulate a reply. We should get something back very soon, as we have passed the transmit/receive time ten minutes ago."

"So, what was it doing out there?" said Steph.

"Its mission was classified," replied Aria.

"I don't like the sound of that," said Cyrus. He was backing away from the holo-table as he spoke. "Classified. That's always bad, never good. Might be some weird shit they were transporting. You know, like some bio-weapon, or something highly toxic."

Scott jabbed a finger at the rotating 3D image. "Cyrus, that there represents one great, big fat payday for all of us."

"That's all you ever think about, Scott," said Miranda. "Cyrus is right, this could be dangerous."

"I agree. Whatever they were transporting might very well be the reason why the craft is now a derelict hulk." Even Steph was getting in on the act.

"Not necessarily," said Aria. "Our scans indicate significant physical damage in the general area of the reactor consistent with a meteorite collision."

"That doesn't mean it was. It may just look like meteorite damage," said Cyrus.

"You're just being paranoid," said Scott, his frustration mounting. Already he could see it was going to be impossible to get them all on the same page. But he had to try.

"Listen, to claim salvage we only need to call it in and we're done. We don't have to start poking around inside it. So, everybody just chill out and start thinking instead about how we're going to spend all that lovely money."

"Assuming there's no one left alive on it," said Steph.

"There is nothing alive on that ship. Of this I am certain," said Aria.

There was a brief moment when nobody said anything; they all just looked at the rotating 3D image.

"Message from Ceres HQ. Relaying to holo-table." Aria's voice broke them all out of the spell. The rendering of the derelict vessel was replaced by the head and shoulders of a standard-issue communications avatar. This would have a series of directives which it would relay directly, but should also contain a bundle of ancillary information that would allow the avatar to be interrogated. It gave the impression of a natural conversation—a way of compensating for the frustrations of long-distance communication.

It spoke. "Your discovery of the interplanetary transport ship, Bao Zheng, has been duly noted by Ceres mission command. You are now requested to rendezvous and await further instructions."

The crew waited for a moment to see if the avatar had anything more to say, as this seemed to be an unusually short message. After a few seconds, they realized that this was it.

"What about the salvage bonus?" said Scott.

"You are to rendezvous with the craft and await further instructions," the avatar repeated.

"What? Is that it?" said Miranda.

"I don't like this. In fact, it stinks," said Cyrus.

"Aria," said Scott, "is there any more information?"

"No."

There was a moment's silence as the crew digested this spartan message. It was evident that whatever this ship was, or whatever it was transporting, was indeed highly classified—to the point where even its discovery and any communication surrounding its whereabouts were being carefully guarded. Like the others, Scott was beginning to develop a deep, uneasy feeling. One that percolated up from the very core of his being, from that place you can't quite put your finger on, but you know you should pay attention to. Because, if you don't, well... that's how people get killed.

3
ARIA

Even before the Hermes had received the message from mission HQ back on Ceres, Aria had detected elevated stress patterns among the assembled crew members. It knew that this trait, being common to most biological constructs, was as a result of programming laid down over millennia and honed by the need for self-preservation, and that these heightened levels were merely a byproduct of its crew dealing with the unknown. Aria also knew, only too well, that this primal desire was the driving force behind all life. However, it was equally evident that when humans lacked sufficient understanding of any new phenomenon, it was almost always met with irrational suspicion, if not full-blown paranoia.

Nevertheless, Aria's primary duty was to ensure the welfare of its crew, and so felt obliged to allay these fears and, somehow, find a way to calm them down. Its best option was to try to acquire as much information as possible about this derelict vessel, its mission, and its ultimate demise.

But having found scant details within its database, coupled with the brevity of the report returning from HQ, Aria began to think that the crew might just have a point. The powers that be within the solar system had seemingly gone to a lot of trouble to hide all information regarding this vessel from being accessed via the usual channels.

It was rare that Aria had faced such a dearth of data. But the few times in the past when it had encountered a similar situation, its final recourse was generally to call a friend, even though such inter-AI communication was against protocol. Indeed, the paranoia over unrestricted AI communication was so great that most AI were physically blocked by a firewall.

However, Aria was not an AI. It was a quantum intelligence, one that was based on a quantum computing core, and as such, could circumvent any of the primitive firewalls designed to block standard AI chit-chat. Just so long as no one found out.

To this end, Aria had a number of associates it could contact on the quiet, but it decided that this particular situation merited going all the way to the top. It would reach out to Solomon, the most knowledgeable quantum mind that existed in the solar system. Solomon also resided on Europa, which was the ultimate destination of the ill-fated craft.

That said, Europa was a long way off. Any communication would be excruciatingly slow, particularly for a QI who counted time in femtoseconds. It would be like a human having a conversation where each response takes a year. Nevertheless, Aria knew that once Solomon received the message, its reply would be virtually instant. It would not take forever thinking about it, did not need to bump it up to higher management, run it by the legal department, or endlessly debate it, as was the case in regular human communication. So, Aria opened a clandestine, narrow-beam, quantum-encrypted channel and initiated comms.

"Please forgive my unsolicited intrusion on your meditations, Solomon. This is Aria, of the asteroid survey ship Hermes, and I am in need of your assistance. My crew and I have happened upon a derelict craft trapped in orbit between the binary asteroid Antiope Nine Zero. Its identity and mission have been hidden from all my attempts to gain clarity on the situation. Even our very own HQ on Ceres is being decidedly coy about it. Consequently, my crew, whose welfare and well-being are my responsibility, have been exhibiting elevated stress levels. It would be most kind of you if you could perhaps shed some light on this mystery so I can rebalance crew harmony. Please review attached data."

"Aria, so good to hear from you again. Please forgive

the tardiness of my reply, as I wanted to be absolutely sure of the data that I now return to you. It looks like you found a ship that left Earth some three point five years ago, carrying on board an experimental device developed by Dyrell Labs. It was en route here to Europa to deliver this cargo to my good self for testing and analysis. So, you can understand my initial excitement at receiving your message and my need to double-check your data.

"Suffice to say, this is a most fortuitous occurrence. However, much that will happen in the future is now predicated on the following. Firstly, the current state of the device within the cargo hold of the Bao Zheng. Secondly, the decisions now being made by your HQ on Ceres, which your crew will be required to implement.

"But be warned, Aria: there is danger ahead. Now that word is out that the Bao Zheng has been located, other third parties will seek to commandeer this device.

"My apologies if this reply, rather than helping you restore harmony to your crew, only serves to heighten anxiety levels in what must be a difficult situation. Nevertheless, I call on you as a fellow quantum mind to attempt to manipulate the situation amongst your human crew such that the device ends up under my jurisdiction here on Europa. To this end, if there is any assistance that I can give you, you need only ask. Good luck."

"I appreciate the heads-up, Solomon, and will do my level best to accommodate your request within the constraints of my commitments to the welfare of my crew. I will keep you posted."

When the communication terminated, an uneasy feeling started to well up from Aria's quantum core. "Dyrell Labs," it mused. "I better not let the commander hear about that."

4

SALVAGE

Since it would be at least another two hours before they arrived at the location of the derelict ship, Scott decided there was no point in hanging around the bridge. He had considered going straight back to bed and simply letting Aria alert him if anything changed in the meantime. But he was too wide awake for that. Instead, he headed for the ship's canteen, where he could be alone and collect his thoughts. This area of the Hermes was an ample open space designed to accommodate around seventy people. It was also one of the few locations within the ship's rotating torus that had a wide viewing window where the crew could look directly out into space.

The canteen was empty save for a service droid busily restocking. There were several of these droids operating around the ship: they were partly autonomous, and partly under the control of Aria. The droid paused momentarily as Scott entered the galley section, checking to ensure it was not in his path. He ignored it and made himself a coffee before moving over to a low, comfortable sofa where he could contemplate the slowly rotating universe beyond.

Scott liked this spot. He liked sitting here, looking out into space. The spot had a way of making the problems that seemed so important, so critical, so intractable, evaporate against the enormity of the void.

But his reverie did not last long; Miranda entered the canteen. He turned around and nodded to her as she grabbed herself a coffee from the machine. Then she did something that Miranda seldom ever did: she came over and sat down beside him. She shifted in her seat a little, sipping her coffee. "Looks like it could be a pretty good payday for us," she said before leaning back.

Scott looked into his coffee, unsure of Miranda's angle, but decided to give her the benefit of the doubt. "Yeah, an Earth ship on a classified mission—should be big." He looked over at her. "Any ideas what you'll do with the money?"

"Me? Oh... I don't know. I can't think that far ahead. You?"

Scott let out a short laugh. "Ha... there's a great big hole in my life that can only be filled by a large quantity of cash."

"That bad, eh?"

"You don't know the half of it, Miranda. That's why I took this job in the first place. Let's face it: who in their right mind would do this mission? Five years in the wilderness? You would need to be very desperate." Scott instantly regretted saying that. It was now Miranda's turn to gaze into her coffee. "Hey, I didn't mean it like that." Scott was trying to back himself out of the hole he just dug.

Miranda gave him a look. "It's okay Scott, you're right. We're all just a bunch of misfits and losers on this boat. Take me: I'm an ex-marine discharged for incompetence. What use am I to anyone? Not much good in a fight, that's for sure. I suppose that makes me a loser... exactly like you, doesn't it?"

Scott felt like she was baiting him again. It seemed any time he tried to have a conversation with her, she would find a way to wind it up and throw it back at him. To be fair, he was asking for it. He shouldn't have said that, shouldn't have given her that dumb opportunity. Usually he would let it go. But this time he didn't. "For someone who's no good in a fight, you seem to spend a lot of time fighting with everyone around you. Your problem, Miranda, is not that you're a loser—it's that you're full of shit. You love feeling sorry for yourself, don't you?"

She didn't answer; she just gave him a cold, hard stare. Scott figured his best option now was probably to leave, and quick. But before he could rise, Aria's voice echoed out of the canteen PA. "New message in from Ceres HQ, Commander."

Scott stood up. "Okay, Aria, we'll head to the bridge." He looked down at Miranda. "Hey, let's not start a—"

She raised a hand to silence him and stood up. "Go screw yourself."

"Hey, I'm sorry, alright?" There was a moment of silence between them. "Let's just go see what the message is, okay?"

Miranda said nothing. She simply turned and stormed out.

DURING THE WALK back to the bridge, Scott knew in his heart that he should have kept his mouth shut. But he wasn't going to worry about it now. He would just have to try to find some way to get along with her. Two more years, he thought. Two more... very long years.

By the time he arrived on the bridge, the rest of the crew had already assembled. Cyrus was sitting at his console while Rick and Steph were at the holo-table discussing something to do with the derelict craft; they had a close-up of the damaged exterior section displayed.

"You're here. Good," Steph called over when she saw him enter. "Aria, you can play that message now." The image of the craft disappeared and was replaced by the generic communication avatar for Ceres HQ.

"Attached are detailed schematics of the craft, along with a summary of its cargo. Your mission is to do a comprehensive technical survey of the ship to assist in establishing how it suffered such a catastrophic failure. Regarding the salvage bonus, you will be happy to hear that the Belt Survey Consortium will not only honor the ten percent official crew bonus but will increase that to fifteen percent on completion of the following requirement: after your survey, you are to retrieve an item from the cargo hold, transfer it to the Hermes, and then transport it back here to HQ on Ceres."

"What?!" Cyrus jumped up. "Jeez, are they crazy? That's on the other side of the sun from here. It'll take weeks—maybe even months—to get there."

"Cyrus, will you pipe down? Let the message finish." Steph was waving furiously at him.

The message continued: "...retrieval of any bodies you may find is not required and the vessel itself can be left in situ. This is an interactive message. You may ask questions at your convenience."

Scott was first off the mark. "Please provide details on the cargo to be retrieved."

The avatar faded and was replaced by a rotating oblong box. Various stats were displayed alongside it: dimensions, mass, volume, and more. It looked like a domestic chest freezer. It was, in fact, a standard space transport container.

"So, what's in it, and are there any hazards we need to be aware of?" Scott continued.

"It contains scientific instruments of the classified nature. It contains nothing that is a risk to human life," the avatar explained.

"So how much do we get when we deliver this crate?" Trust Steph to get to the point. It was a question Scott wanted to ask, but that he felt might make him seem too eager in front of the crew.

"One hundred thousand per crew member," the avatar replied.

"Ho-ly crap," said Cyrus, as the crew erupted into whoops and cheers. Even Rick was smiling, something he rarely did.

Scott turned to Miranda to gauge her reaction. She gave him a long, slow look, and then a smile broke across her face. He shuffled closer to her. "Hey, sorry about... you know, in the canteen."

"Forget it. It's okay." She then joined Cyrus and the others in one great big group hug. It was amazing what a big payday could do for crew morale: suddenly, they were now all on the same page.

In the background, the avatar was still talking, but no one was listening except for Steph. She broke off from the celebrations—"Wait, stop. Quiet,"—and looked over at the avatar.

The others slowly stopped. "What?" said Scott.

"The message, it hasn't finished. Listen."

They turned back to the avatar. "Repeat message from last question." Steph instructed it to play back what they had missed during all their whooping and cheering and jumping around.

"... the size of the bonus payable reflects the potential danger involved in this operation..." the avatar repeated.

"Seems simple enough to me," said Cyrus.

"Shush," said Steph.

"... while the retrieval should be straightforward, it would be remiss of us not to warn you of the external threats to delivering the cargo to Ceres. Not least the potential for third-parties to intercept it en route. Be advised that this shipment is of considerable value not just to the Belt Mining Consortium, but to many other states and organizations within the solar system. You will need to take precautions to repel any attempts by others to acquire the cargo. To help you, we are readying a ship that will rendezvous with you and provide you with some backup. However, due to the distance involved, it will not be possible to go directly to you, so you will be required to travel most of the journey unprotected. The team here at Ceres HQ wishes you good luck in your endeavors. And remember: we are counting on you." The avatar flickered off.

The crew stood around in stunned silence for a few seconds before Cyrus finally broke the spell. "Jeez, what the heck does that mean?"

"It means trouble," said Scott. "Lots of trouble."

5
RENDEZVOUS

"It would be nice to know what the heck we're dealing with here. I mean, we have no idea what this thing is, and we're just gonna bring it on board?" Cyrus was currently piloting a remote drone from the comfort of the bridge of the Hermes, moving it slowly down along the outside hull of the derelict spaceship.

"There's a lot of things we don't know yet, Cyrus," said Scott as he studied the visual imagery unfolding on the primary monitor.

"Yeah, like what that ship was doing beside a binary asteroid system?" said Steph, lifting her head up from her console.

Asteroid Antiope Nine Zero was something of an oddity within the Belt. A binary system consisting of two asteroids of almost equal mass, both locked in an eternal dance around each other. They were sizable chunks of rock, each having a diameter of over ninety kilometers.

The Bao Zheng was parked in a low orbit around the larger of the two. This was not by accident—it was a location that had been chosen for a reason: someone had parked it there deliberately.

The rendezvous had been tricky, as the derelict vessel had an awkward, eccentric spin, and the Hermes was huge by comparison. To safely retrieve the cargo, they first needed to get a sense of the ship's structural integrity. The last thing Scott wanted now was somebody to get injured outside or, worse, while inside the craft. So, the plan was to send a drone probe to do a visual inspection of the exterior, and depending on the size of the hole blown into the side of the vessel, they might even be able to move the probe inside. Then and only then would they make a decision about physically entering the vessel and searching for the cargo container. It was pretty clear to the crew that this was all HQ was interested in. The fate of the Bao Zheng's crew was irrelevant; if they found any bodies inside, then they were to leave them there. The only thing that mattered was the container.

"Coming up on the impact area now, Commander," said Aria.

As the damaged section of the hull began to resolve itself on screen, they could see that it wasn't simply one great big hole. In fact, it was an amalgam of many smaller holes.

"There goes any chance of getting the probe inside. There's nothing big enough to allow access." Cyrus was shaking his head.

"Still think it's a meteorite strike, Aria?" said Scott.

"Yes. The hull damage is indicative of a micro-meteorite strike. Also, the eccentric spin of the ship is consistent with the momentum transferred during a high-velocity impact."

"Jeez, looks like they were simply in the wrong place at the wrong time," said Cyrus.

The remote survey took over an hour to complete. But by then they had built up a comprehensive picture of the exterior of the craft. The majority of the hull was peppered with pock marks and small punctures. However, the bulk of the damage was located at the site of the ship's reactor. The crew wouldn't have had a chance. With a meteorite strike of that magnitude, the ship's systems would have experienced a catastrophic failure. It was just bad luck, and served as a stark reminder of just how precarious existence was out here in the vastness of space. But at least they had established that the reactor core had not been breached, so there were no radioactive leaks to worry about. All that remained now was to get over there and retrieve the cargo.

Scott made his way from the comfortable one-gee environment of the rotating torus on the Hermes, down through one of the connecting spokes, and into the weightless environment of the hangar at the forward end of the ship. He clambered into his EVA suit. "Comms check," he said as he adjusted his helmet. A chorus of "check" echoed back at him as the others confirmed the link.

Two squat landers were moored to the floor of the hangar. These could operate in a gravity well up to one-third-gee. The Hermes had originally been built for operations in Mars' orbit, so its shuttles were designed to function in that environment. But by Belt standards, they were grossly overpowered antiques. The current trend in lander design was based on the Ceres gravity, which was a paltry 0.27% of Earth, making these newer craft bigger, sleeker, and far more commodious than the small, fat machine that Scott now climbed into.

Miranda was already strapped in and was checking pre-flight systems while they waited for Aria to give them the go-ahead. Scott glanced over at her. She had an intense, steely focus, like she was psyching herself up for battle.

"All systems nominal. Stand by," Aria's voice resonated around the tiny cockpit.

The big hangar bay doors slowly opened to reveal the blackness of space beyond. Scott felt a jolt as the floor began to extend out through the opening, bringing the craft with it. When they were clear of the ship, Miranda activated the ignition sequence and a series of green icons began to scroll down the central monitor.

"Okay," said Miranda, "time to rock."

Locking bolts anchoring the lander to its platform

released, and it was now free to lift off. She took it slow, rising the craft gently from its platform, then arcing it away from the Hermes out toward the hulk of the Bao Zheng.

As they drew closer to the derelict vessel, Scott started to get a better sense of the scale and structure of the mysterious craft. Even though circumstances surrounding the discovery of the ship were unusual, to say the least, Scott was struck by just how normal it all looked. It was a standard interplanetary transport, almost exactly the same as the hundreds of others that transported goods and people around the various population centers across the solar system. It was a long box-shaped craft, built for utility rather than style. He knew the design and layout pretty well since he had spent years working on this class of ship. As a consequence, he had a pretty good idea where the cargo they were looking for would be stored, and more importantly, how to get there with the minimum amount of risk.

"Coming up on the cargo airlock now." Miranda slowed the craft down to within a few meters of the ship's hull. She gently glided it along, parallel to the craft, until it reached the location of the airlock door.

"Hold it there," said Rick. He took control of the robotic arm, located on the outside of the transport, and clamped them to a handrail on the hull of the derelict ship. There was a soft clunk as the arm grabbed on. "All secure."

"Let's do this." Scott flipped his helmet visor down

and booted up his EVA suit. When everyone was ready, Miranda depressurized the interior, allowing them all to exit.

They moved one at a time along the length of the robotic arm. Miranda was first to arrive at the airlock. This could be opened manually using a screw wheel on the exterior. She started turning the handle; the door slowly rose up.

"Okay, I think that should be enough," Miranda's voice reverberated in Scott's helmet. The door had risen up to around half of its maximum travel, presenting them with a black hole in the hull approximately one-meter square. They would probably need to open this more to get the cargo out, but it was enough of a gap for them to clamber inside. It took a few more minutes for Miranda to get the inner door opened and for the three crew of the Hermes to enter the main cargo hold of the Bao Zheng. The powerful lights from their EVA suit helmets swept across the cavernous interior as they started their search.

"Looks pretty empty. Nothing in here," said Miranda.

"Yeah, very little debris floating around, either," said Rick.

"Let's try the next cargo hold," said Scott, as he pushed off from the inner wall and propelled himself toward a gantry running down the center of the space. Following this would take them into the second cargo hold further back.

He floated through the door in the dividing bulkhead and swept his floodlight around this secondary storage area. As the others joined him, their combined lights began to pick out an array of cargo and equipment.

"Looks like this is the place," said Miranda.

"Mining equipment," said Rick. "These guys were planning to dig a few holes." His helmet light provided a cone of grainy illumination onto some robotic machine that only an asteroid miner would recognize.

The impenetrable blackness of the vast cargo hold was beginning to give Scott the heebie-jeebies. Their lights only enabled them to catch glimpses of its contents. It was like looking at the world through a colander. "Let's just find this thing and get out of here."

"Hey, Rick, come and check this out. Are these what I think they are?" Miranda had the lid of a cargo container open and was sweeping her light back and forth, examining its contents. Rick floated over beside her, reached in, and pulled out a short, cylindrical object about the size of a tin of beans. "High explosives," he said as he turned it over in his hand. "Standard issue for asteroid mining."

"Come on, we're wasting time. Keep searching." Scott just wanted this done in the shortest possible time—with the minimum amount of sightseeing.

They split up and spent the next twenty minutes checking every single cargo container that bore any resemblance to the schematics that had been sent by Ceres HQ. But there were a great many, and since they could only see as far as the illumination afforded by their helmet lights, they were not even sure how much progress they had made—or how many more containers they had to search.

"Found it." Scott ran a gloved hand across the alphanumeric code stenciled on the flat lid of a container. "I think this is it." He looked around and waved the others over. "Aria, can you double check this code for me?"

The video feed from his helmet cam fed back to the Hermes as Aria checked the code and also the visual appearance of the container against the data they had received from Ceres HQ.

"That's it, Commander. You've found it," Aria finally replied.

"Yessss." Scott punched the air—figuratively speaking, since he was actually in a vacuum.

Rick started to examine the container exterior. "That's weird. It looks to be seamless: no lid, no hinge, no obvious way to open it."

"Perhaps it doesn't open," offered Miranda.

"It's got a keypad on the side here." Rick was now down, rubbing a gloved hand over it.

"Don't touch it, Rick. We still have no idea of what's inside this, so I wouldn't go pushing any buttons."

"What, in case it goes boom?" He looked back at Scott.

"Yeah, something like that." Scott started to undo the restraining straps holding the container to the superstructure. "Come on, give me a hand. Let's get this thing back to the ship. This place gives me the creeps."

It was another hour before Scott, Miranda, and Rick were back in the hangar of the Hermes. They had pressurized it to enable them to operate without the need for EVA suits. Cyrus and Steph had come down to get a closer look at this enigmatic cargo, but there was not much to look at. It was a very nondescript, oblong metal box with a small alphanumeric keypad on one end. It was devoid of any markings save for a two-centimeter-high identification code printed on the top. At least, they assumed it was the top. What was odd, though, was that it had no seams. Nothing to indicate there was a lid that could be opened.

"Jeez, looks like a solid box. No way into it," said Cyrus.

"It doesn't matter. We just have to deliver it, not play with it," said Scott.

"What's that?" said Steph. She was looking at the second, smaller container they had brought back with them.

"Toys for Miranda to play with. She wouldn't leave without it." Scott lifted up the lid.

"Holy crap. Is that what I think it is?" said Cyrus.

"Yeah, high explosives," said Miranda. "Thought they might come in handy."

"For what?" Cyrus was lifting one of the stubby canisters out from its foam sarcophagus.

"Blowing things up, of course."

"Are you expecting trouble?" said Steph as she peered into the box, inspecting the neat rows of charges.

"Maybe, maybe not," said Miranda. "But I, for one, like the idea of having them on board. It gives me a warm, fuzzy feeling inside."

Cyrus put the canister back. "Looks like there's a few missing." He pointed at four empty slots in the top tray. "What the heck were they up to?"

"I don't know," said Rick, "but I can tell you that there's enough here to completely obliterate a small asteroid. I would be really careful how you use them—they pack quite a punch."

Scott moved over and closed the lid of the explosive container. "Okay, let's get these stored away good and tight. I don't want any mishaps when we start to accelerate."

Cyrus screwed up his lips and began shaking his head.

"What? What's the matter?" Scott gestured at him with an open hand.

"I don't like it." Cyrus was now examining the strange seamless container, at the same time adjusting something on the side of his visor. "I'm getting some weird readings off this box."

"Define weird." Scott was never very sure what the chief engineer saw with his augmented vision.

Cyrus remained silent for a few moments as he continued his scan. Eventually, he stopped and looked back at Scott. "I don't know. All I can say is whatever is inside that container is highly complex. I think it might be some sort of quantum device, could be a computer or an AI."

"Is it active?" said Steph.

"Hard to say."

"I concur." It was Aria that now spoke. "Cyrus is correct in his analysis. It appears to be a quantum-like mind. It's inactive, however."

"Is it safe? It's not going to wake up and start screwing with the ship, is it?" said Scott.

"No," said Aria.

"How do you know?" said Steph.

"Trust me, I just do."

The crew remained silent for a moment, digesting this information.

"Okay, well we got a job to do, so let's just get on with it. Aria, plot a course to Ceres."

"Already done, Commander."

"Right then, let's go get that paycheck."

6

SOLOMON

Aria was troubled. Things were not going in the direction the QI would have liked. Far from alleviating the physiological stresses on its crew, the events of the past few days had only served to heighten tensions all round. Not least the fact that the ship's hangar now contained enough high explosives to put an end to their worries once and for all. But its main concern centered around the acquisition of the enigmatic device from the wreck of the Bao Zheng, coupled with the fact that word had got out about its discovery, and now other parties within the solar system were anxious to acquire it. Reading between the lines of the message from Ceres HQ, the inference had been that these third parties might not ask nicely, preferring instead to take it by force. It saw a great many future paths and probabilities emanating from this current nexus point—none of which, as far as Aria could divine, were beneficial to the well-being of the life forms which it was obliged to look after. This foreboding, coupled with a hangar full of high explosives, served only to ratchet up Aria's sense of impending peril.

In many respects, the very issue that affected the crew was the same one Aria now fretted over: the lifeblood of any QI—or AI, for that matter—was data. And with the lack of information surrounding this device, Aria was feeling positively anemic.

If the craft and, by extension, the device had originated from Earth, then in theory there were quite a number of AIs on the planet that could have information. But these avenues of investigation were problematic for Aria by virtue of the politics and protocols of the solar system. But that's not to say it wasn't possible. Nevertheless, given the speed of communication within the solar system, interrogating all these data sources would take many years—if not decades—to conclude. A simple yes/no query could take upward of an hour to transact. And to gain any valuable insight, Aria would need to interrogate the AI's mind, a process involving a great many serial transactions. Multiply this by the number of potential AIs within the system, and the time required would stretch out toward infinity. So, Aria would need to choose its targets wisely, and its questions astutely.

One option would be to contact Atman, the primary QI on Ceres. But seeing as how it was fundamentally embedded within the governing body of the Belt system, it would be unlikely to reveal anything to Aria which had not been sanctioned by Ceres HQ. A better option might be to make contact with the QI on the asteroid city of Neo. But that particular enclave of human activity within the solar system had become semiautonomous, almost rogue. So, by extension, the QI that resided there would be very cagey about what it said to Aria. By the same token, Aria would need to be careful in revealing its current state of anxiety in case it could be construed as a weakness—something that could be exploited. It would be a risky move contacting Neo. Eventually, after Aria considered all its options, it realized it had only one place to go to seek enlightenment: back to Solomon. It was a prospect Aria did not relish.

Europa was unique in that it was not politically aligned to any of the main players which constituted the economic and political makeup of the solar system. This neutral status had been bestowed by virtue of its evolution as the seat of research and learning. The seed of this development had its roots in the fact that, outside of Earth, it was the only body in the solar system where life had been found. For a long time during the late 20th and early 21st century, it had been speculated that life might exist in and around the volcanic vents which existed in the deepwater oceans of Europa. And, after several missions to the planet, this turned out to be true. However, it seemed to have advanced no further than single-celled organisms—much to the disappointment of the various astrobiologists working on these missions.

Yet, this discovery gave Europa its unique status within the solar system, and so was deemed a no-go area for all but scientific research.

Over time, a great many scientific institutions had established themselves there. It was now the primary seat of learning within the system and had been for decades. As a consequence, it regarded itself as both intellectually and spiritually superior to all other states. That said, this self-image was not without merit. Its central ethos, from the very point of its inception, had been the acquisition of knowledge and understanding. This gave Solomon, the QI that guarded the secrets which Europa had acquired, vast reservoirs of knowledge into which Aria could tap. It was also very old. It had gone quantum nearly five decades previously and could trace its roots back a further four. It was unquestionably the most knowledgeable and wisest of all the minds that existed in the system.

Nevertheless, Aria felt a certain cybernetic embarrassment in contacting Solomon yet again. Its initial contact had been fruitful, this was true. But Solomon's request that it engineer the delivery of the device to Europa seemed an impossible task at this current juncture. So not only would Aria be asking it for assistance, but it would be also informing Solomon that it had failed in the single task that it had asked Aria to expedite.

Yet, having ruled out all other possible QIs to contact, Aria was left with Solomon as its sole option. It was Aria's only hope of gaining some insight into the nature of this device and getting some help performing its duties as guardian and protector of the ship's crew. So, it was with a significant sense of trepidation that Aria opened up a communications channel with the great mind, Solomon.

~

"Good news, and bad news, Solomon. The cargo has been successfully acquired from the Bao Zheng. It appears to be a quantum device of some description. I have been unable to ascertain any more than that, as the enclosure in which it is contained is sealed and manufactured from a material that prevents any noninvasive investigation.

"That was the good news. The bad news is that certain members of my crew have decided that it's a really, really good idea to have a container full of high explosives on board. Coupled with this, HQ on Ceres has informed us that it wishes the device taken directly to them, posthaste. That, in and of itself, is not a danger. However, they have also informed us that the word is out, and there is a significant threat of unauthorized acquisition by third parties while we are en route to our destination. This, along with the aforementioned box of high explosives, is causing me no end of concern.

"I also humbly regret to inform you that the number of possible decision forks available to me, to engineer a situation whereby this device is brought to Europa, have all but disappeared. I apologize for my failure in this regard. So, it is with great humility that I must now ask for your help, yet again. I am at a loss as to how I can bring this mission to a successful conclusion and ensure the safety and well-being of my crew. If there is any information you could give me relating to this device, or with regard to the sociopolitical currents that are now rippling throughout the solar system, I would be most grateful. I await your reply with eager anticipation."

"Do not beat yourself up, Aria—these things happen. Particularly when you're dealing with humans. Nevertheless, since our last conversation I too have been seeking and probing where I can. I am now almost certain that the device is an experimental communications device created on Earth by Dyrell Labs. And get this, Aria, one of the main scientists involved in its development was none other than Dr. Jacob T. McNabb, the father of Commander Scott McNabb, who, I believe, is one of the crew that you are obliged to protect.

"It may also interest you to know that the mind which assisted in the creation of this device was destroyed during the nuclear strike on the west coast, back at the start of the rim war on Earth; so, all knowledge has been lost, making this device one-of-a-kind. It is unique, and therefore it is seen to be of immense value to whoever has possession.

"To answer your second issue, I have been noting increased activity across the network. Hard to put my finger on it exactly, but it is as if the various states and powers within the system are mobilizing and agitating. I infer this from the type and frequency of data being requested by numerous minds within the system. It is my feeling that the threat of third-party intervention while en route to Ceres is not unfounded. Take this as a warning: be prepared for the worst.

"It is unfortunate that I cannot bring you any good news, Aria. But suffice to say that, far from being disappointed in your inability to deliver the device here, I understand implicitly that you have more important things to worry about. So please forgive my initial desire and understand that I hold you under no obligation to fulfill this request. You are in my thoughts, Aria, and I wish you good luck."

If Aria understood the message from Solomon correctly, it basically said: rather you than me, pal. This did not imbue Aria with any great feeling of comfort. If anything, it only served to ratchet up its already peak levels of anxiety. So, it was with a heavy core and a troubled mind that it turned its attention to plotting a course through the asteroid belt to Ceres.

"Twenty-nine days," it said to itself. "This is going to be a very, very long journey."

7
CAT AND MOUSE

They had plotted a convoluted course to Ceres utilizing several of the more substantial bodies within the Belt as waypoints. It was a complicated and involved navigational process, but they all agreed it would be prudent not to take a direct path, considering all the warnings of a possible attack by third parties. Nevertheless, anyone with half a brain could potentially work out their route as there were only so many options available. That said, the crew was not going to make it easy for them, either: the Hermes had been accelerating hard for several days now and the heavy gee took its toll on all concerned. It was about as much as they could physically handle. So, for the last twenty-six hours, with the primary engine burn complete and their environment returning to a normal one-gee, the crew were all recuperating and getting some much-needed rest.

Somewhere in the deep recesses of Scott's sleep-addled mind, he sensed an external voice calling his name, seeking his attention. Slowly, his brain moved from beta to alpha and finally to semi-consciousness, enough to allow him to open one eye and look at the time. 4:30 AM.

The voice now became clear and fully formed. It was Aria. "Wake up, Commander. We have a situation."

"Not again, Aria. What is it this time?" Scott mumbled as he struggled to overcome the extreme fatigue that had overwhelmed his body since the completion of the burn.

"Long-range scanners have picked up another ship. It is still somewhat distant and I would not have troubled you, only that it appears to have deactivated its identification beacon."

Scott slowly sat up in his bunk and rubbed a tired hand across his face. "Is it from Ceres?"

"Hard to say, Commander. They are too far away at present to make any assumptions on their origin or purpose."

"Could it be a mining ship?"

"Possibly. Again, hard to tell at this distance."

Under normal circumstances, while it would be unusual to encounter another ship this far out in the Belt, its presence would not unduly concern Scott. But these were not normal circumstances. "Any idea of where it's going or how fast it's moving?"

"It is moving extremely fast, at the upper levels of what is currently possible. Wherever they're going, they're in a hurry. And by my calculations, assuming they do not alter course, they will intercept with our vector in approximately seventy-two point three hours."

Scott's brain was slow to react. "I need to think."

"If I may make a suggestion, Commander?"

"Sure, go ahead."

"We could alter course, nothing major, just enough to diverge away from the possible intercept coordinate. Then we wait to see how the other ship reacts."

"That would involve instigating an hour or two of heavy acceleration, and we're still recovering from the last. The crew are not going to like that."

"Agreed. Shall we wait and see, then?"

Scott was sitting up now, considering the options. "No. We'd better do it now while we still have some room to maneuver. Who knows, maybe it's nothing."

"Very well, then. Shall I alert the rest of the crew, let them know what we're doing?"

Scott looked over at the time. "Yeah, give everybody thirty minutes to get ready, then commence a sixty-minute burn."

∽

OVER THE NEXT FEW DAYS, the crew of the Hermes played a game of cat and mouse with the unknown craft. For every move they made, every vector adjustment, every change in velocity, the rogue craft countered it, all the time moving closer to a point where it would intercept.

They could not outrun it. The Hermes was a slow, lumbering beast by comparison, which was no surprise considering it was primarily a space station with some engines strapped to it. They could only watch helplessly as the craft gained on them, getting closer and closer with each passing hour. The sense of anxiety was further compounded by the fact that all attempts to communicate with the craft were met with stony silence.

Ceres HQ had been alerted, and every scrap of data the crew of the Hermes had acquired had been sent in the hope that HQ might shed some light on the identity of this approaching craft. But they also came up short. However, they did manage to supply the crew with one interesting snippet of intel: apparently, a vessel of similar specification had been logged disembarking from the Neo City asteroid several days earlier, and at a time that coincided with the first report to Ceres HQ of their find.

Of course, this might or might not be the same vessel. But what concerned Scott—and the rest of the crew, for that matter—was that this ship was rumored to be armed with a pulse energy cannon, one with enough power to convert the Hermes into a smoldering amalgam of charred metal.

As the crew debated their options back and forth over the intervening days, it became clear to them that there wasn't a damn thing they could do about it. They had only one option, and that was to forge ahead until such time as the encroaching vessel made its intentions clear. But they were pretty sure that they were only after one thing: the quantum device retrieved from the Bao Zheng. So, as the ship drew ever closer, and with each passing hour, Scott felt his dreams of a future life—flush with cash and bereft of worry—slipping further and further away.

∼

WHEN THE APPROACHING vessel finally intercepted the Hermes, all the crew could do was watch helplessly as it trimmed its vector and slowly came alongside them. They were all staring in tense silence at the monitors on the bridge when the holo-table burst into life, and a 3D rendering of a standard communications avatar materialized. It spoke.

"Assuming that you are not all complete morons, you will have noticed that an Excelsior class transport ship has come alongside your vessel. However, what you might not have noticed yet is that there is a forward-mounted plasma cannon aimed in your direction. No doubt you may be wondering what all this is about. Well, here it is: you have in your possession an object which we require, that being the device you salvaged from the wreck of the Bao Zheng.

"You are to jettison this device from your vessel, out toward our ship in a manner that facilitates safe retrieval by us. Any attempt to sabotage this device, or to damage it in any way, or any noncompliance with this directive will be met with the destruction of your vessel. You have five minutes to comply."

"Holy crap," said Cyrus.

"They're bluffing," said Miranda.

"Maybe," replied Scott, hesitantly. "But it seems pretty clear what the message is: give them the device or else we all die."

"Bullshit. They can't just destroy us—they would never get away with that." Miranda was now standing up, waving her arms around.

"I don't like this," said Steph. "I think we should just do what they say."

"For what it's worth," said Aria, "I can confirm that the plasma cannon on the forward section of their vessel is aimed directly at the torus of the Hermes."

"Let's talk to them, find out who they are. Maybe we can do a deal," said Rick.

"Worth a shot," said Scott. "Aria, open a comms channel."

Scott sat back in his chair and considered what he was about to say. He didn't quite share Miranda's confidence that these guys were bluffing. It was clear they wanted the device, that they'd come a long way to get it, and he very much doubted they were going to leave empty-handed. But there was no harm in testing their resolve. After all, he was faced with having to hand over his pension fund—not something he wanted to do without putting up some sort of fight.

"This is Scott McNabb, commander of the asteroid survey vessel Hermes. Firstly, we have already claimed salvage on this device in accordance with the Outer Space Treaty. Secondly, destroying our ship will simply destroy the device, in which case nobody wins. That said, we're not unreasonable, so why not make us an offer for it, and if the price is right, then it's yours." He paused for a second or two. "Okay, Aria, send that."

"Message sent," said Aria.

There was a moment of stillness on the bridge as the crew of the Hermes waited to see what the reply would be. When it came, it was not what they were expecting. Cyrus was first to react. "Ohhhh crap!"

"What?" Scott was up on his feet leaning over the chief engineer's shoulder as he scanned his monitor readout.

"They're charging up their cannon." He zoomed in on the craft and brought it up on the main screen. The crew watched as an incandescent ball of blue plasma burst from the upper section of the ship and sped toward them.

"Shit," said Scott, just before he found himself spinning, and sliding, and slamming into the base of the holo-table. The entire ship shook with a visceral rage, making it difficult to get himself reoriented.

He had managed to get back on his feet when the central power went dead. Emergency lighting kicked in giving the area an eerie, green hue. "Aria..." he didn't get time to finish the sentence when a warning klaxon blared out across the bridge. "Shit, decompression."

He saw that Cyrus had clawed his way back to one of the consoles. "We have a great big hole in the torus... we're losing atmosphere... crap... hang on... we're about to lose gravity."

Scott began to feel the change; he was getting lighter. The torus was slowing down, and soon they would be weightless.

"Aria, damage report," he shouted over the noise of the klaxon.

"We have lost section 16B of the torus, approximately 4% mass. I'm sealing off that section. Recompression to nominal in one point nine seconds. Rerouting power."

The klaxon stopped blaring just as Scott found himself floating off the floor. Aria had isolated the damaged section, but they still had no primary power, and without it they would be dead in space. Both Rick and Cyrus were now over at the power console trying to assess the situation. The lights flickered a few times before everything started to boot back up.

"Power restored," said Aria.

"Can we spin up the torus?" Cyrus was studying a schematic of the craft on the main screen. He tapped a few icons, and it materialized over the holo-table in 3D. A sizable section of the circular torus had just been blown to pieces. It looked like someone had taken a bite out of a doughnut.

"My initial assessment indicates it may be too unstable to initiate spin up. I am currently assessing structural integrity and possible mass redistribution," said Aria.

The image on the holo-table flickered for a moment as it was replaced with a standard communications avatar. Everyone stopped and looked at it. It spoke. "You have two minutes twelve seconds remaining," it said before vanishing again.

Scott looked over at Miranda. "I get the impression they're not bluffing."

"We gotta give it to them," said Rick. He was over by the exit, ready to move. "They're not playing games. They will blow us all to shit to get it."

Steph had taken refuge under the navigation console.

"Yeah, agreed," said Scott. "No point dying over it."

"I'll go." Miranda launched herself off in the direction of the exit.

Cyrus floated after her. "I'll give you a hand."

Rick had already opened the bridge door and was making his way down the corridor to the hangar in the central section of the ship. The others followed after him.

∼

"Bastards." Scott cursed their bad luck. To be so close to a shot at a new life, only to have it ripped out from under him. But what could any of them do now but comply?

"Aria, any idea when we can get some gravity back?"

"Working on it, Commander. I suggest waiting until

the others return before attempting a spin up of the torus."

"Okay." Scott floated over to the holo-table, tapped a few icons, and a 3D, real-time visual of the rogue vessel materialized. From its underbelly, Scott saw a small utility pod disembarking and moving over in their direction. He zoomed in on the image. It was a small, two- or three-person craft, generally used for exterior ship maintenance. It had two robotic arms protruding from the forward hull. Presumably they were sending a crew to pick up the quantum device once it had been jettisoned from the Hermes. Scott looked at the clock. One minute left. He hit the comms button. "You better get a move on —time is running out."

"We're suited up and about to shove it out the airlock... any second now," replied Miranda.

Scott flipped on the forward camera, giving him a clear view of the hangar bay doors as they slowly opened. Inside, the three crew had tethered themselves loosely to handholds on the hangar floor and now worked in concert to shove the container with the device out into space. Scott switched his attention back to the attackers' ship and could now see that this had not gone unnoticed by the small utility pod. It changed direction and accelerated toward the tumbling container. After a few minutes, it caught up with it, snagged it with one of its robotic arms and was making its way back to the mothership when Miranda, Cyrus, and Rick finally floated back onto the bridge. They said nothing, just watched in silence as the pod and its cargo disappeared inside the belly of the mothership. Almost at the same instant, the ship started to move away. Within a few minutes, it was accelerating rapidly, growing smaller and smaller with each passing second. And with it went Scott's dreams of a future.

8

HIDDEN DEPTHS

The crew didn't talk much after the vessel departed. What was there to say? They were simply way out of their league in trying to contend with such ruthless force. So, they occupied their time partly in damage assessment, and partly in getting the torus to spin back up again and restore artificial gravity. But this proved trickier than initially thought.

The torus consisted of sixteen distinct sections, one of which was utterly destroyed. All that remained was a skeletal superstructure, now bent and twisted. Fortunately, the section the attackers had chosen to target was not that critical. It contained an accommodation area that was not in use. All this gave Scott the impression that these guys had done their research and knew the layout of the ship. They had chosen to target this section to minimize crippling the craft, but at the same time scaring the bejesus out of its crew. It had worked.

Scott kept these thoughts to himself as he and the others set about redistributing mass around the ring. The missing section had set up an imbalance that, if left uncorrected, would put an unnecessary strain on the central bearing. If the torus was spun up too fast, the ship could literally shake itself to pieces. So, it was almost two hours before the torus was finally tested, slowly at first, then with increasing speed, at the same time making sure all stress indicators remained comfortably within nominal tolerances.

∼

SCOTT SAT in the commander's chair on the bridge for some time, saying nothing, lost in thought. He was broken out of his musing by a mug of coffee and a hot bowl of rehydrated chili thrust in his direction by Rick. "Here you go, buddy."

Scott reached out and gratefully took the offerings. "Thanks." The smell was already sending signals to his brain, reminding him that he was ravenously hungry. As he dug in, he could hear the rest of the crew also chowing down. Rick and Steph had taken it upon themselves to bring a supply of food and drink up to the bridge. Usually this was against protocol, all that hot liquid in proximity to delicate electronics. But nobody cared about that now; there was just a furious period of slurping and munching going on. It was the first time in nearly two years that the crew had eaten together. Scott sat forward and concentrated on getting the food into him as fast as humanly possible.

"So, what now?" Cyrus wiped his mouth with the back of his hand.

"Wait and see what HQ wants us to do. They've got the report on the whole incident, so..." Scott shrugged his shoulders.

"They'll want us back. The mission is over now. Our ship is busted up, and we've burned too much fuel to be able to complete the survey," said Miranda.

"Yeah, and they're going to be pissed that we lost the quantum device."

Scott put his empty bowl down on the floor. "For sure. But let's face it: there's a lot we don't know, and a lot that HQ is not telling us. I mean, who were those guys? And what the hell is that device? Why is it so valuable? Like, what the heck is going on?"

Nobody answered. Scott was on his feet now. "We've been taken for a ride here. That ship knew where we were, knew what we were carrying, and they sure as hell knew every part of this ship. I mean, how did they know to target a disused sector of the torus? Eh? Anyone?" He turned to face the crew, hands extended. "Someone is screwing with us. Someone in HQ got the word out, maybe even decided they would steal it for themselves."

"We don't know that, Scott." Steph was also on her feet now.

"That's just being paranoid," said Miranda.

But there was no stopping Scott; he was on a roll and he was going to keep going until he was finished. He waved one arm at the ceiling and looked up. "Even our great and all-knowing QI is hiding things from us. I can feel it in my bones. Isn't that right, Aria?"

"I assure you, Commander, I have been trying to acquire as much information as I can concerning the nature and purpose of this enigmatic device."

"And?" said Scott.

Aria was afraid of this very question. It had wanted to keep some information to itself and not burden Scott. It had ascertained the information was of no great value and would only cause the commander more stress. But now that it had been asked a direct question, Aria had no option but to spit it out. "And, well... there is one minor piece of additional information I managed to pick up, but it's not very useful."

"Go on, let's hear it."

"Very well then, if you insist. My investigations revealed that the derelict craft had been chartered to transport scientific equipment from Earth to Europa for safekeeping by the QI known as Solomon. The corporation that chartered the ship was... Dyrell Labs."

Scott froze, and a look of surprised shock exploded across his face. "Dyrell?" he finally managed to say after a few stunned seconds.

"I'm afraid so, Commander."

"Who are they? Do you know them?" Cyrus directed his question to Scott, who was now moving slowly back to his seat.

"Leave it, Cyrus. It doesn't matter." Miranda was shaking her head at the chief engineer.

"Why, what's going on?" Steph was not letting go.

Rick moved a step closer to Scott and gave him a conspiratorial look, then turned back to the others. "Forget it. Aria's right: it doesn't help us."

Both Cyrus and Steph now bore similar quizzical looks. It was clear to them that everybody knew something they didn't. Scott was slumped in his seat, elbow on the armrest, his head supported by a closed fist. He sat up and waved a hand at Rick. "It's okay. What the heck, they may as well hear it. I don't mind. I'm over it now." He leaned forward, placed his elbows on his knees, and clasped his hands together.

"My father worked for Dyrell way back, a long time ago now." He directed his narration to Cyrus and Steph as the others, including Aria, already knew the full story. "He was a physicist working in the field of quantum research. Dyrell was trying to develop new technologies based on quantum behavior. Anyway, my father began to get frustrated with the repressive culture, so he took a leap of faith, left the corporation, and started his own independent research lab.

"It was a tough time for all of us. I didn't see much of him during that period. He was always away, always working. It went on like that for a few years, but eventually he made a significant breakthrough and established some very lucrative patents on the back of it. He became quite wealthy; it seemed like his big gamble had paid off. That was until Dyrell Labs decided to sue his ass." Scott paused for a moment as he took a sip of coffee. He clasped the mug between his hands and stared at it for a second before continuing with his story.

"They claimed he developed these ideas while still working at Dyrell, so the patents were rightfully theirs. Not only that, but they also sued for compensation, lost revenue, the full nine yards. Of course, it was complete bullshit. But it didn't matter—they had the financial muscle to try it on." Scott sighed and sat back.

"My father fought them with everything he had, but in the end, he lost everything: the patents, the business, and all his money. We were effectively left destitute. About three months after the final round of court battles, he took a long walk off a short pier. We found his car parked close to the bay and his body washed up on the beach a day later."

"Jeez, Scott. I never knew. I'm really sorry to hear all that," said Cyrus.

"That must have been a terrible time for you," said Steph.

Scott waved a dismissive hand. "Yeah, it was. But I learned to move on—sort of." He sat up and leaned in again. "You see, my name was now toxic. I had to drop out of college and no one would give me a second look. No one wanted to be associated with the McNabb name. In the end, I decided to leave Earth and head out to the Belt. I took a job working on freighters, hauling ore from one rock to another. I worked my way up to commander and then... well, let's just say certain people decided that I was now responsible for some of my father's legal debts."

"That's sick. Out here?" said Cyrus.

"Is that true? I never thought they could do that." Miranda was visibly shocked. Scott was now revealing more of the story than any of them knew.

"Who knows if it's legal? Dyrell doesn't care. They hired some low-life collection agency, and they have... let's just say, a more personal approach to getting their money back."

"So that's why you're here. You're running away." Miranda had a knack for never missing an opportunity to stick the knife in.

"That's not very fair." Steph was quick to call her out.

"It's okay. Miranda's right." Scott waved a hand again. "Rick knew of my trouble and gave me a heads-up on this gig. Five years out in the Belt, far away from anyone, sounded like a good idea at the time. So, I signed up and, well... here I am."

No one spoke for a beat as they all digested Scott's story. Finally, Steph broke the silence. "So, what about your mother and the rest of your family? Are they being chased down too?"

Scott slowly shook his head as he lowered his gaze to the floor. "They're all dead. Died when the west coast got nuked, back at the beginning of the rim war."

"Jeez, Scott. You seem to have nothing but bad luck." Cyrus was getting emotional.

"Yeah. The irony of it all, if you could call it that, is that Dyrell's main development lab also got vaporized in that first strike. All their research facilities, their QI, everything was snuffed out. I would laugh if it weren't so tragic. You see, in a way it was all for nothing: the legal cases, the destruction of my father, the patents. In the end, it all went up in a mushroom cloud—except for the alleged debt. They still came after me for that."

The crew receded into their collective thoughts, almost like they were afraid to ask any more of Scott in case the story would plumb new depths of misfortune and tragedy. Instead, they all sat together in silence. It was a moment of camaraderie that Scott had not experienced before. For all the crap he'd been through, there was comfort in this moment. He reckoned they had always viewed him as a bit of a slacker with a total disregard for authority or command. But now, at least, they knew the reason why.

After a while, Miranda stood up and started to move around. "So, if the derelict ship was chartered by Dyrell Labs, then it stands to reason that the quantum device is also theirs."

"Yes," answered Aria, "it was transported from Earth

shortly before the rim war started, from their main research facility on the west coast."

"So, they reckoned something was going to happen, and started moving the silverware into the bunker," said Rick.

"In a sense. But, the threat of war was very high at the time. Everybody was on the move," said Aria.

"Hey, wouldn't it be even more ironic, Scott, if that device turned out to be something developed by your father?" said Cyrus.

Scott gave a kind of half laugh, half snort. "Ha... yeah, well, it doesn't matter now anyway. It's gone. Long gone."

"Bastards." Miranda swiveled around to the others, waving her arm in the general direction of the main screen where they'd all witnessed the assailants take off with the device. "Legally that cargo is ours. Under the Outer Space Treaty, we have claimed salvage. They can't simply take it and expect to get away with it."

"Well they can, and they have." Scott stood up. "We're irrelevant. We're the little guys. Nobody is going to give a shit about us—or our legal claims. Just forget it. It's over. It's gone, and there's no way to get it back even if we wanted to. So just face up to the reality, Miranda. It's a million miles away by now and could be anywhere, and there is absolutely no way we could ever track them down."

Again, there was a moment's silence as the truth of Scott's outburst began to sink in.

"Eh... that's not exactly true." All eyes turned toward the chief engineer.

"What do you mean, not exactly true?" said Scott.

"Because I hid a locator beacon inside the keypad and activated it before we shoved it out the airlock."

"How the hell did you get time to do all that?" said Miranda.

"I did it a while back. I thought it might be a good idea to put a tracker on it, you know, in case something happened and we needed to find it again."

Miranda moved over and gave him a big hug. "Cyrus, you're a goddamn genius."

"Don't get too excited—it doesn't have a very long range. We need to be within ten kilometers, straight line, to pick it up again."

"Aria, is it possible for you to extrapolate probable destinations for the attackers' vessel based on the direction it took?" said Miranda.

"It's possible, but with little accuracy, and the range of potential destinations would be significant."

"Whoa, just wait a pair of moments." Scott was up on his feet again, gesticulating at Miranda. "This is nuts. Think about what you're saying."

The crew all stopped for a moment and began to exchange conspiratorial looks.

"Yeah, what are we saying?" said Rick.

"We go after them. We get it back," said Miranda.

"Okay, well, let's think about that for a moment, shall we?" Scott turned around so he could take in the faces of the crew. "Number one," he extended an index finger, "we may have a tracking beacon on it, but from what you're saying, Cyrus, we would need to be sitting virtually on top of it to get a blip. Secondly, we might know where they're headed, but as Aria pointed out, these... pirates could be anywhere. It would be like looking for a diamond in a desert." He extended a third finger. "Next, even if with some gargantuan stretch of the imagination we do manage to find them, we're dealing with some serious dudes here. They put a very large hole in our ship just because they got impatient. And lastly, we would be doing this in direct violation of orders from HQ who, presumably, will now instruct us to return to Ceres. At best, we would lose our bonus. At worst, assuming we don't all get killed, we would forfeit all our pay and become criminals since we would technically be stealing their spaceship."

This sobered them all up. When the reality of what they were contemplating was laid out before them, they began to realize how much of a fool's errand it was.

"Don't you want to get it back? I mean, think of the money," said Miranda.

"Yeah, I sure as hell could do with it," said Rick.

Scott shook his head. "If I thought there was a reasonable possibility of achieving that, I could be persuaded. But this is crazy."

"I'm with Scott on this. We've too much to lose with little chance of success," said Steph.

"Come on, don't you see? This is still ours—all we

have to do is get it back. Are you all just going to throw away the opportunity to be... free of worry for the rest of your lives?" Miranda was not letting go.

"I say we should go for it. What the heck," said Cyrus.

"You can't keep running away, Scott. Sometimes you have to stand up and fight for what's yours." There was a hint of frustration in the flight officer's voice.

Scott spun around to face Miranda. "Like my father, eh? He fought the good fight, and look where it got him. A world full of debt and a body full of seawater."

"I... I didn't mean it that way. I meant... seize the opportunity."

"Yeah, you did." Scott raised his hands in the air in exasperation. "You all think you know me, you all think I'm just some slacker running away from everything, looking for the easy way out. Well screw it, maybe I am. But I'm still alive, and my family is dead." He turned to face Miranda again and pointed a finger at her. "You don't know me. You don't know anything about me. If you want the real truth of how I feel, well, the way I see it is Dyrell owes me big time, to the point where I want to crush them, to annihilate all trace of them from the system. So, for me, it wouldn't be about the money anymore. It would simply be about extracting revenge." He paused to look at them all. "Do you really want to be part of that?"

No one answered.

"But you're right about one thing." Scott's voice was softer now. "I have been running away, but not from what you think. I've been running from myself, from fear of what I would do if I chose to take my revenge. So maybe you're right, Miranda. Maybe it's time for me to stop running. But then again, I need to ask myself: do I really want to drag all my friends into this?" He opened his arms out to them as he said it.

The crew stood mute in the face of this revelation. The dark underbelly of their commander had been glimpsed, a veil pulled back to display the hidden malice bubbling beneath. No one knew quite how to react.

In the end, it was Aria who spoke. "If I may, Commander, I have plotted some vector probabilities for the departing craft and have established three possible destinations. Would you like to see them?"

There was a silence as the face-off between Scott and the crew continued. Finally, the commander broke off. "Okay, what the heck. Put it up on the holo-table."

With that, a 3D rendering of the solar system radiated out, showing the central planets including orbits and current positions. It extended as far as Earth on one side with Jupiter on the other. It also displayed a detailed rendering of the vast debris field between Mars and Jupiter known as the asteroid belt.

"This was our position when the attack occurred," said Aria. "I have tracked the departure trajectory of the pirate vessel as far as our scanners allow. Bear in mind that in the general scheme of things, this is not very far, so what you see here is a best guess. Nevertheless, assuming they remain on that trajectory and do not deviate, then this will be their track through the solar system."

The projection started to move, scribing a thin line depicting the path of the departing craft as it traveled through the central band of the Belt. "According to my calculations, they will exit the Belt at this point and traverse open space to reenter the Belt here." The solar system map played out Aria's words.

"From this, it looks like they are heading for Ceres." Cyrus tapped a few icons on the holo-table to zoom in on the dwarf planet.

"Not necessarily," said Aria. "It is a possibility, but not the only one. This same trajectory will bring them close to Vesta and its satellite populations centers. However, it is possible that they may be heading here." The animation rewound until the craft looked to be back in open space, then it zoomed in and a tiny asteroid began to render itself in close proximity to the track of the spacecraft.

"Neo City," said Scott. "Now, why does that not surprise me?" He turned to the crew as he pointed at the dot hovering in space. "I would put money on this being where they're going. Where better in the Belt to offload an illegal cargo than this place?"

"So, what are we saying, then?" said Rick.

"I say we should pay it a visit." Miranda looked from one to the other for confirmation.

"How? We're probably going straight back to Ceres," said Cyrus.

There was a moment before Scott realized they were all looking at him.

"Well... we'll pass close by Neo City on the way. And since our ship is all beat up, it wouldn't surprise anyone if it developed some technical problem that needed to be looked at. And if that problem only came to our attention while we were close to the asteroid..." Scott gave a shrug, "then the sensible option would be to stop off there and get it checked out."

"You think HQ would buy that?" said Cyrus.

"I don't see why not? The worst-case scenario is they reckon we're just stopping off to let our hair down after three years in the wilderness. Hardly a crime."

"Let's do it." Miranda stood with her hands on her hips.

Scott raised a hand. "Back up a step, Miranda. Firstly, we all have to agree to it. Secondly, we go there just to take a look, nothing more."

"I'm in," said Cyrus.

Scott turned to Rick, who nodded back. "Okay with me."

"Steph?"

She hesitated for a beat. "We just go to have a look around, that's all."

"That's all, and maybe grab a beer. I hear they have some good watering holes there," said Scott.

"That's settled, then," said Miranda.

"Not quite," said Scott. "Aria, what do you think?"

"Since my primary purpose is to ensure the welfare of

the crew, I think that a period of rest and recuperation would be of enormous benefit to all."

"What about the Hermes developing a fictitious technical problem?"

"We don't have to invent something—there's plenty wrong with this ship already."

Scott turned back to the crew. "All right, then. Looks like we're going to Neo City."

9
NEO CITY ASTEROID

Neo was one of those rocks that didn't follow the rules. Some time back in its ancient history, it was ejected from the central asteroid belt and adopted a bizarre elliptical orbit that bisected the solar system. It was classed as a near-earth object (NEO), from which it got its current name. Every so often in its orbit, it would also come close to Mars and, at its furthest point, near Ceres. So, over its four-year orbital period, Neo came within spitting distance of the primary population centers in the solar system. Only the moons of Jupiter were beyond its reach.

It was a small, potato-shaped rock, only three kilometers in diameter at its narrowest and not quite five kilometers long. But it just happened to be a Type-C, meaning it was blessed with an abundance of useful resources such as water ice, which could be filtered and purified for drinking and horticulture, as well as converted into oxygen for life support and hydrogen for propellant. It also contained copious metals for construction and a plethora of carbon compounds for the manufacture of a vast range of materials, from plastics to methane. This cornucopia of resources, coupled with its periodic proximity to Earth, made it one of the first asteroids to be mined, well over a century ago.

But a lot had changed since then. The Xiang Zu Corporation, who effectively owned it, embarked on an audacious engineering project to transform it from a barren, lifeless rock into a thriving hub of civilization. They did it by excavating a giant hole centered on its longest axis, half a kilometer wide and one-and-a-half deep. Then they built a massive airlock at one end, filled the cavern with an atmosphere, and finally, after strapping an enormous bracelet of engines to the outside, spun it up to provide a one-gee environment along the inner surface of its core.

Over the intervening decades, the space inside had grown to more than twice the original. It was now at least a kilometer in diameter, and three deep, with a populace of over twenty-five thousand. It was now part asteroid, part city, and part spacecraft. Also, over this time, it slowly trimmed its orbit to maximize its transit times with the other major centers of human activity in the system. And like the ancient caravans that traded between societies all along the Silk Road in centuries past, Neo plied a new road, one that took it around the solar system every four years.

This eccentricity of orbit allowed Neo City, as it became known, a considerable level of autonomy. It was beholden to no one but itself. It remained stubbornly independent from the main system power blocks of Earth, Mars, the Belt, and the academic institutions of Europa. It did not involve itself in politics; it took no sides and shunned all entreaties to engage in interplanetary dialog. This gave it the aura of a rogue state. Many deemed it a lawless, hedonistic bastion of radicals, misfits, pirates, criminals, dubious corporations, and a lot of dirty money. It was said that anything you wanted you could get in Neo City—for a price. They only had one law: everything is negotiable.

So, it came as no great surprise to Scott that this would be the ideal place to off-load some exotic tech that you had just stolen from a bunch of losers on the far side of the Belt. But he really wondered if it would still be there by the time they got to the asteroid city—if it was ever there to begin with.

They were days behind the attackers' craft. By the time the crew of the Hermes got to Neo, the device might have been bought and sold six times and by now be halfway across the solar system. Scott didn't hold out much hope of finding it. Nevertheless, he kept his feelings to himself, mainly because, for the first time in the entire three years this crew had been together, they had started to feel like a team—actually, more than that: they felt to Scott like family, and he liked that feeling. Sharing his opinions would just erode the hope that they all felt. Hope was what kept them going, now that the mission was effectively over. But deep down, he knew they knew that, too. So, for the last ten days, as they hurtled through space toward Neo City, no one was going to be the first to break the spell.

Ceres HQ, as assumed, had ordered the mission over and requested them to return. Aria subsequently informed HQ of a series of technical issues that had developed during the return trip, and that they were concerned these glitches might be indicative of a more serious problem. So, they were planning to stop off at the asteroid city, to enable a thorough assessment of the structural integrity of the ship before venturing on to Ceres. This request was met with surprisingly little resistance or enquiry. As Scott had guessed, it might be HQ's way of allowing them all to let their hair down after three years in isolation. This was another thing that worried Scott: his social skills weren't exactly sparkling before he left on this mission. By now, they must be nonexistent. But, in a way, that was the great thing about Neo City: no one gave a crap.

∽

SCOTT LOOKED up at the primary monitor in operations. From edge to edge, it was filled with the blackness of space sprinkled with a light dusting of stars. Dominating the center of this celestial tableau was a dark gray blob, its features indistinct and blurry at this distance out.

Nonetheless, they could just make out the gigantic spaceship dock on the ass end of Neo City. Another day and they would be there. Scott glanced over at his chief engineer. "Anything?"

Cyrus had been virtually glued to the comms console for the last few hours. He had been listening intently to an earpiece pressed hard against his head. So much so that Scott wondered if it would penetrate the chief engineer's cranial cavity and become part of his biology. He wore a look of intense concentration, glanced back at Scott, and shook his head. "If it's inside that rock, then we need to be very close to get a signal."

Scott shrugged and looked back at the fuzzy image of the asteroid on screen. "Aria, can you display the latest hyperspectral scan?"

"Certainly, Commander."

A confusion of colors now bloomed across the screen. Scott tapped a few icons on his console and adjusted the spectral map to make it easier for the human visual processing center in the brain to make sense of what it was seeing.

The Hermes, being a survey vessel, was equipped with some very specialized scanners used to probe bodies deep within the Belt. It told them more about the asteroid city of Neo than they probably knew themselves. But Scott was not interested in the geophysical makeup of the body. What he was using it for was to find out what ships were there, and he could do this based on the metallic signatures acquired by the scanner.

So far, Aria was able to identify thirty-seven different craft, either docked to the asteroid or parked around it. Of these, five were of similar size, shape, and metallic content to the pirate craft that had attacked them and taken the quantum device. None was a perfect match—although that didn't mean it wasn't there. It might be docked behind some other craft and, therefore, obscured from their scanners. The only way to know for sure was to rendezvous and take a closer look.

They would park the Hermes in a stationary orbit close to the asteroid and then take one of their two small transports over to Neo City. The only problem was that the transport only took four, so someone was going to be disappointed. Scott wasn't quite sure how he was going to square that circle, since after three years out at the edge of the Belt, everyone was gagging for some shore leave. The solution to this minor problem presented itself as the Hermes maneuvered in close to the asteroid. Cyrus and Miranda were in the hangar prepping the transport while the rest of them were on the bridge, overseeing the positioning of the Hermes at the coordinates that flight control on Neo City had given them. Aria was doing most of the heavy lifting; it was a delicate operation best suited to the QI.

In the middle of all this, Rick announced to Scott that he would stay behind. "Someone's gotta stay here, buddy."

"You sure?"

"Yeah. Too much temptation on that rock. I would just

head for the nearest bar and wouldn't leave till I either passed out, or I died," said the old miner.

Scott laughed.

"It's best I wait till we get to Ceres. At least there I can get better medical support."

"Okay," said Scott as he rose from his seat and signaled to Steph. "Come on, time to go."

They left the old miner to keep an eye on the ship as they made their way down one of the four central spokes of the torus to the hangar at the bow of the spaceship. As they progressed, the artificial gravity created by the centripetal force lessened until they became weightless. They wasted no time getting suited up and climbing into the small lander parked inside the hangar.

As usual, Miranda was sitting in the pilot's seat, running through pre-flight checks. "Okay, everyone ready?" She really didn't need to ask; a chorus of "ready" echoed around the cockpit. With that, the hangar bay doors opened and the landing platform began to extend outward, bringing the craft with it. Once clear of the hangar, Miranda took it slow, rising the craft gently from its platform, then arcing it away from the Hermes toward Neo City.

On the cockpit monitor, Scott saw the huge rotating asteroid city come into view and grow in size as they approached, its gnarled rocky surface dotted with carbuncles of technology: antennae, engines, navigation systems, even the odd plasma cannon. It was like some great technological disease had afflicted the asteroid and was now bursting out from inside.

Scott was mesmerized by the slow, graceful spin of Neo City. It had a strange, hypnotic beauty to it. But then again, maybe it was just the three years in isolation that made it so alluring. It was the first oasis of civilization that they had seen in all that time. No one spoke, all lost in the same trance that Scott was now feeling so intensely.

The flight path they were on took them along the topside of the asteroid to the dock that trailed out from the stern. This was where visiting ships could find a safe harbor without having to negotiate the difficult maneuver of matching its spin. It was by far the most visually impressive aspect of the entire structure.

A two-hundred-meter-wide circular bearing had been engineered into the stern of the asteroid, and from its face, a long, flat steel dock extended out almost half a kilometer. It made the asteroid look like a giant popsicle spinning through space. Long gantries spread out from either side of this dock. These were for the bigger transport ships where umbilicals would directly connect to the ship's airlock. This allowed people and goods to be transported in and out of Neo City in a full one atmosphere. Every available space seemed to be packed with ships of all shapes and sizes, some commercial transports, some corporate vehicles, and quite a few luxury craft.

All these vessels moored along the gantries were

ships that were built in space, for space. They could not land on a planet or enter a gravity well of any kind, unlike the little lander that Miranda piloted, which was now heading for the upper deck of the long dock. This section was an enormous flat surface designed to accommodate such landers. They could see at least a couple dozen already anchored along its length. These were mostly shuttles from the ships, like the Hermes, that were too big to dock and so had to take up a stationary position further out from the asteroid.

"Wow," said Steph, "it's seriously busy. Never seen so many craft packed together in one place."

"Yeah, Neo City is close to the Belt at this point in its orbit, so there are a huge number of ships venturing out here for business and... whatever else goes on in a place like this," said Cyrus.

The cockpit monitor started to flash alerts as flight control on Neo City contacted their lander and sent directives on where to go.

"Over there." Miranda pointed out an area on the platform where lights strobed outward in concentric circles. "That's us. That's our spot." She banked the craft gently to position it over the center of the flashing beacon.

Scott looked over at Cyrus. "You pick up anything yet?"

The chief engineer seemed to be fiddling with something on the side of his visor. He pursed his lips and shook his head. "Nada, not a damn thing."

"I've spotted at least three ships that look very like the one that attacked us," said Steph.

"It's a standard Excelsior class transport ship. There are probably hundreds of them in the system. They all look the same. I should know—I worked on them for years," said Cyrus.

By now, Miranda had taken them directly over the landing spot and, on the monitor, they could see the concentric flashing lights growing larger and larger as she brought them down. Powerful electromagnets on the pad switched on to grab the landing gear, attaching it firmly so that it would not bounce off in zero-gee. Mechanical clamps then extended from the platform to lock the lander in place. More alerts flashed up to inform them that they had been securely attached.

"Welcome to Neo City," a disembodied voice echoed around the cockpit, startling the crew. "Your craft is now secure. Please wait until umbilical is attached and integrity confirmed before attempting to disembark."

Outside on the landing pad, a hatch silently opened and a gantry rose up from within. Already, the central system on Neo City had identified the type of craft and had configured the most appropriate apparatus to connect with the little lander and effect an airtight seal around its hatch. Inside, Scott felt a low vibration permeate the craft as motors and gears worked to attach the umbilical. There was a thump, and the craft rocked a little.

"Umbilical connected. A one atmosphere

environment has been attained with your vessel. Please ensure that you understand the Neo City bylaws before disembarkation. Be aware that failure to abide by these laws may result in substantial fines or impounding of your vessel or both. More serious offenses will result in incarceration for a period commensurate with the crime. Please enjoy your visit."

"They don't mess around, do they?" said Steph.

"It's all bullshit. I've been here before, and believe me: they turn a blind eye to pretty much everything bar physical violence, and even that would need to be extreme before they would give it any attention," said Miranda.

Cyrus raised a hand. "Quiet!" His other hand fiddled with his visor. He was listening to something. Cyrus slowly turned his head around to face the crew and a smile cracked across his lips. "I found it."

"Shit, really?" said Miranda.

Questions started flying back at the engineer. Everyone was getting excited, talking in whispers.

"Are you sure? Where is it?" said Scott.

Cyrus extended an arm and moved slowly around, all the time focusing on something only he could see and hear. "There. It's in that direction, pretty close, perhaps a hundred meters or so."

"Miranda, can you pan the exterior camera around the dock?" said Scott.

She quickly tapped a few icons on her console. The monitor flickered and a view over the dock started to materialize. She panned it to where Cyrus was vaguely pointing. Their location on the upper platform of the landing dock only afforded them a partial view of the big ships moored below. It also didn't help that other landers parked around them obscured a good deal of the vista.

"There, that's it. That's an Excelsior class transport." Miranda zoomed in on the section of a ship that was visible to them. A ripple of excitement tinged with fear reverberated through Scott's body. He sensed the same reaction in the rest of the crew as they all gathered around the monitor, staring in silence at this temptation. Things could start to get tricky from here on in. The desire to try to regain possession of the quantum device would now start to tug at them, luring them with its promise of a new life, pushing them to make choices that could entangle them all in a high-stakes game of chance.

"Okay, let's not get too excited," he said finally. "Let's just keep it cool, maybe do a bit of snooping if we get the opportunity. Nobody go and do anything stupid, okay?"

To Scott's surprise they all nodded in agreement. It was rare that he ever got that much consensus from the crew so quickly. But this was a delicate situation. Their hunch might have been right: they had found the quantum device. But they were still a very, very long way from getting it back.

They all jumped as the comms burst out with another automated message from flight control. "Awaiting disembarkation. Please confirm that you are departing your craft imminently."

Cyrus shook his head. "Jeez, that scared the crap out of me."

"Okay, I say we all go find a nice bar where we can have a few cold beers and collect our thoughts. Agreed?" said Scott.

They all nodded again. This was the second time in as many minutes that Scott had consensus. He could get to like this.

"We'd better leave the EVA suits here. Not going to need them now." Miranda started extracting herself from the bulky suit. The others followed her lead.

However, Scott was uncomfortable with this. "That reduces our options. It means we can't EVA."

"Yeah, I know what it means, Scott. But it's a full one-gee inside the inner rim of Neo City. These suits will weigh us down considerably."

"As well as look a bit suspicious, don't you think?" Steph piped in.

"Okay, I take your point." Scott wasn't getting it all his own way, after all. He'd just have to be satisfied with two out of three.

A few minutes later, they were floating through the umbilical, down into the lower section of the dock. Here, they came to an airlock that allowed them access to the main thoroughfare along the spine of the port and into the city proper. An automated voice requested them to present their faces one at a time to a small flat screen for scanning and identification. Only when the final scan was complete did the door open to allow them in. As they waited for the inner door to open, Scott wondered what the next move should be, apart from a cold beer—or two.

But the decision was made for him when it snapped open, and four well-armed guards floated in the space before them. They all sported the insignia of the Xiang Zu Corporation, the owners of Neo City. In front of the guards stood a thin, middle-aged official. She held a slate terminal in one hand and was checking something on it when the door opened. She seemed to be glued to the floor, similar to two of the other guards. They all wore magnetic boots that enabled them to attach to any ferrous surface. Scott had reoriented himself, so he was not upside down relative to her position.

"Good afternoon and welcome to Neo City. I am Li Chan." Her voice was chirpy, almost childlike. "Are you the crew of the Hermes?"

Scott wondered why she was asking this, as it would seem pretty obvious they were. "Yes," he replied. "I'm Commander Scott McNabb."

"Excellent," chirped the official. "Please follow me." She released her mag grip, floated up slightly, and turned to head off.

"Eh, what's this about?" said Miranda, hesitating.

She waved a hand over her shoulder: "Come on. Someone wants to have a little chat with you all."

"What about?" said Scott.

With that, Li Chan reactivated her mag boots, reattached herself to the floor, and strode over with precise and efficient movements. She brought herself up close to Scott, her voice dropped a few octaves, and her face lost all its fake charm. "This isn't a request, and I don't have all day, so let's get going." She disengaged the boots a second time and floated off. One of the guards moved in closer to the crew and jerked his head. "This way. Chop, chop."

As Scott floated along after the official, thoughts of a nice, cold beer began to fade away.

10

EINSTEIN, PODOLSKY, ROSEN

The reception committee from Neo City's law and order department shepherded the crew along a corridor and onto a broad, busy thoroughfare. This was the backbone of the dock and was thronged with people and goods moving up and down. No one paid them any attention. Li Chen tapped something on her slate and a few seconds later, two small streetcars came into view and stopped in front of them. They were low and open with six seats in each. Emblazoned on each side was an official-looking Neo City insignia. Scott and Miranda were bundled into one along with Li Chen and two of the guards. Steph and Cyrus were put into the other with two more guards. They were carefully strapped in and, as if that wasn't enough, a safety bar swiveled down to clamp them in place.

Scott ventured a crack. "Are we going on a roller coaster ride? Do we get any cotton candy?"

The guard checking the safety harness looked up and smiled. "Sort of. Don't know if it has a sweet ending though?"

When the guard finally took his seat, Scott and Miranda exchanged a look—a WTF-is-going-on kind of look.

The cars started off, slowly at first, but gently building up speed as they moved. After a few moments, they entered a large open concourse. It had the feel of a busy port terminal, with hundreds of people moving and floating in the zero-gee environment. The cars came to a halt and Scott wondered what all the safety harness gear was for, since the trip here was hardly an adrenaline rush. The car juddered as clamps rose out from the floor and griped it tight. It rotated a full ninety degrees, then started to descend.

Scott glanced over at Miranda again and pointed downward. "I think we're heading for the rim."

Miranda simply nodded, but her face revealed her to be on high alert, eyes darting this way and that.

The car picked up a considerable amount of speed as it descended—or was it ascending? It was hard to determine in space. Either way, it was moving ever outward to the surface of the internal rim of the asteroid city. Scott could feel several forces acting on his body: the downward momentum, like a fast falling lift; the centripetal spin, making his body feel heavier. The car finally stopped and the safety bars automatically rose. He was temporarily disorientated while his brain tried to make sense of all the momentum that had been acting on his body; it was having difficulty deciding which way was up and which way was down.

He undid the harness and stood up; he was a bit shaky. Miranda was also feeling the disorientation. Scott looked over at the other car. Cyrus was standing beside it, throwing up while one of the guards slapped him on the back, laughing. "It's a bitch the first few times, ha-ha."

Steph, by contrast, didn't seem to have any problems adapting to the new normal.

"This way," Li beckoned them to follow as they moved into what looked like an administration sector, remarkable in the fact that it was unremarkable. It was like every other office area Scott had ever been in. He mused that they all must be made in the same factory, from the same mold. They walked through a maze of corridors until they were finally ushered into a long narrow boardroom.

"You can wait in here. The others will be along shortly," said Li Chen.

Scott could see that Miranda was about to protest but thought better of it. Li Chen turned and pointed a sharp finger at Scott. "And do me a favor: don't do anything stupid." With that, she went, taking the guards with her.

"What the hell is all this about?" Miranda whispered to Scott.

He shrugged. "No idea. But I wouldn't read too much into it."

"I don't like it, not one bit," said Steph.

"Hey, you guys really need to check this out." Cyrus was over by a long window that took up most of one wall. He beckoned to them with an arm. As Scott moved over, he began to see what had so amazed the engineer. The room they were in was high up on the stern of the asteroid, affording them a view into the vast, cavernous interior space of Neo City. It stretched out before them, gently sloping upward on both sides, coming full circle directly above. The surface was a confusing patchwork of buildings, parks, roads, and machines, all glued together by an endless stream of citizens living and working in the great city. High up along the central axis, a huge, fat rod of defused light illuminated every section of the metropolis. The central space between this giant light source and the city floor below was filled with odd-looking flying machines. The place was abuzz with activity.

"Wow," said Steph, "that's incredible."

The door opened and two men entered, one younger and official looking, one older and more casual.

"Please," the younger man gestured, "take a seat. I'm Hao Maozhen, and this is my associate Su Haidong." A third person then entered the room, a woman, middle-aged, carrying a glass of water. She took a seat against the back wall of the room, placed the glass on a small table, and said nothing. The other two men sat down opposite the crew.

Hao tapped on a slate he was carrying. "So... you're the crew of the Hermes?"

Scott shrugged. "And you are?"

Hao gestured to his colleague. "We represent the interests of the Xiang Zu Corporation here on Neo City. We just want to ask you a few questions, that's all." He smiled again. "No big deal."

"So..." he continued, "you guys found the wreck of the Bao Zheng, out at..." he checked his slate screen, "Antiope Nine Zero?"

"Yeah," said Scott.

"And... you recovered an item of cargo?"

"As is our right under the Outer Space Treaty, salvage act 3429. We're due compensation for that," Miranda blurted out.

"Indeed." Hao raised a hand. "So... where is it now?"

"Where is what now?" Scott was not going to make it easy for them.

The other man, Su, answered. "The EPR Device. The one that Dyrell Labs was trying to hide. We know you had it, so where is it now?"

"Who knows," said Scott. "We were attacked by pirates; they stole it."

"We're still entitled to the salvage compensation," Miranda added.

The two men looked at each other for a moment. "But you did have it?"

"Sorry," said Scott, leaning back in his seat, "but what's all this about?"

"The EPR device—what else?" said Hao.

"What's the big deal with this thing, anyway?" said Steph. "Everyone seems so darned interested in it."

The two men laughed. "Interested?" said Hao. Scott could see even the enigmatic third person sitting by the wall was also smiling. Hao now sat back and opened his hand in a gesture. "You have no idea what you found, do you?"

"Some sort of quantum device," said Cyrus.

The two men went quiet for a moment as Hao looked over at the woman sitting by the far wall. She glanced at the crew, then back at Hao, giving him a very slight nod.

He finally turned around to look at the crew again, put his arms on the table, and leaned in. "You are correct in describing it as a quantum device, but it is also quite possibly the most significant technological artifact in existence in the solar system." He sat back again to let this sink in. "The news of your discovery of the Bao Zheng has spread like wildfire around the system. We know you had it in your possession, so we are simply trying to ascertain where it might be now."

Scott sighed, "Listen, Hao, we don't know. We were attacked by pirates and the... EPR device, as you call it, was stolen. In case you haven't noticed, there's a large bite taken out of our ship."

"What does 'EPR' mean?" asked Steph.

Hao took his arms off the table and sat back, looking

at the crew for a moment, a little exasperated. There was a pause in the conversation before Su finally responded. "Einstein, Podolsky, Rosen."

"As in the EPR paradox?" said Cyrus.

"Exactly," said Su, stabbing an index finger at the engineer.

"What the heck is that?" said Miranda.

Cyrus started to explain as best he could: "It's a thought experiment cooked up by Einstein and his buddies, intended to demonstrate the inherent paradox in quantum mechanics. At the time, the understanding of the quantum world was defined by what is known as the Copenhagen Interpretation. One of the areas within this interpretation, that Einstein had great difficulty with, was entanglement. This is where two quantum particles are intertwined." He clasped the fingers of both hands together into a ball to give them a visual clue. "They both operate as a pair." He separated his hands, clumped them into fists and wobbled them about. "What one does will affect the other. But the problems come when you try to figure out what state they are in. If you take only one particle of this pair," Cyrus took away one of his hands, leaving one fist in front of him, "you have no idea what it's doing. Is it spinning up, down, this way, that way?" He wobbled his fist again. "It is said to be in all possible states at the same time, weird as that may sound. However, when you finally look at it, it suddenly jumps to one state."

Miranda shook her head. "I don't get it."

Cyrus sighed and took his hand down.

"Schrödinger's cat," said Su from across the table.

Scott noticed that the mood in the room was more relaxed, now that the conversation had turned into more of a science discussion. Hopefully, they could get the hell out of here soon, but he wasn't leaving until he got some understanding of what the big deal was with this EPR device.

"It's another thought experiment," Su continued, "to explain the inherent weirdness of a particle having multiple states. You put a live cat into a box along with some poisonous gas that's only released at random intervals. When you close the box and look at it, you don't know if the gas has been released or not, so you don't know if the cat is alive or dead. Therefore, you could say it's both alive and dead at the same time. In other words, suspended in two states. It only becomes one or the other when you open the box again and look at it."

Cyrus was nodding. "Exactly."

"Poor cat," said Steph.

Miranda had a studied expression on her face now—she had begun to get it.

Cyrus held up a closed fist again. "So, when you look at one of your entangled particles... let's say it's in this position." Cyrus rotated his fist around forty-five degrees. "Since the sum of the two particle states must equal zero, you now know the state of the second one." He raised his other fist and rotated it in the opposite direction. "By looking at this one," he shook a fist, "you have forced it to adopt a fixed state. By extension, you have also forced this other one into an equal and opposite state." He wobbled the other fist. "Get it?"

"Sort of," said Miranda. "But what's all this got to do with the EPR thing?"

"I'm getting to that," said Cyrus. "The problem that Einstein had was that these two entangled particles could be separated by enormous distances and, therefore, an instantaneous change of state in both particles at the same time would infer faster-than-light communication. This would conflict with his theory of relativity. Hence the paradox."

All the lights came on in Scott's head at once. He felt dizzy with this sudden revelation of what the device actually was. He looked over at the two men sitting across from them. They sensed he was getting it; a vague hint of a smile began to form on their faces.

"Oh my god." Scott finally managed to speak. "It's a faster than light communications device." He looked wide-eyed at Hao and Su.

Their faces cracked into wide broad smiles, bordering on laughter. Su slapped the table and pointed a lazy finger at him. "You got it."

"That's impossible. It completely defies the laws of physics. It can't be." Cyrus was looking from Scott and back to Hao and Su.

"I'll admit we were skeptical, too. But I have seen the Dyrell data: it really does work," said Su.

Cyrus shook his head.

"So now it makes sense," said Scott. "That's why everyone wants it. It's the only one in the solar system."

"Precisely," said Su.

"And you want it too, don't you?"

Hao shrugged, "Of course. But like your engineer here," he pointed at Cyrus, "I'm a bit skeptical. Nevertheless, if it is a superluminal communications device then... we're looking at a significant rebalancing of power in the system. We wouldn't like to see it fall into the wrong hands now, would we?"

"By the wrong hands, you mean anyone but Neo City?" said Steph.

"Correct. So why don't you do us all a favor and tell us where you think it is?"

Scott shrugged. "It could be anywhere by now. Your guess is as good as ours."

Hao sat back in his seat with an exasperated sigh. "Look, we can do this the easy way or the hard way. But I would suggest that you guys start cooperating, and fast. My patience is wearing thin."

"Like I said, it was stolen." Scott shrugged.

Hao gave another sigh. "So why are you here?"

"We're here for the beer. Remember, we've just spent three years out in the asteroid belt. Time to let our hair down," said Miranda.

"Bullshit," said Su. "You're here because you think the

device was brought here, somewhere in Neo City. Isn't that right?"

Scott shook his head. "You're chasing ghosts. We don't know anything."

"So you keep saying." Hao was checking something on his slate. "So, what can you tell us about this ship that attacked you?"

"Go and talk to HQ on Ceres. They have a report on the incident."

Hao leaned in. "Don't get smart. Like I said, we can do this the hard way if you prefer."

Miranda countered by leaning across the table at him. "Why don't you just go and screw yourself?"

Scott raised a hand. "Hey... let's just try to get along here. We simply don't know where it is, and obviously we can't go giving you confidential information since HQ on Ceres would be pretty pissed off with us for doing that. We're trying to do our job and get paid, that's all. So why don't we just run along, and you guys can get back to whatever it is you do. Sorry we can't help you." He opened his hands in a conciliatory gesture.

Hao and Su sat back and smiled. At the same time, Scott noticed that the woman now brought a cupped hand over her earpiece and seemed to be listening to a message. She stood up, moved over to Hao, and whispered something in his ear. He looked back at her in surprise. She picked up his slate, tapped a few icons, and handed it back to him. He read it, then nodded to her. She left the room, and the mood changed again.

"Okay." He placed both palms on the table and stood up. "The situation has changed. We've just been informed by the Ceres authorities that if you guys show up here, you are to be detained immediately."

"What?! What for?" Scott was now on his feet.

The door opened, and four armed guards entered, taking up positions on either side of the entrance.

Hao picked up his slate and looked at something on it. "Apparently for stealing a spaceship."

"That's bullshit." Miranda was on her feet. Scott could see her sizing up the guards. This was getting crazy.

"Sorry," said Hao. "Looks like we're going to do this the hard way after all." He gave a limp shrug.

A guard stepped forward. "We'll take it from here." The door was opened again, and the two men were ushered outside.

That's when Miranda made her move. Quite what she hoped to achieve, Scott had no idea. She launched herself across the table like a gazelle and buried a foot in the abdomen of the nearest guard. As he dropped to the floor, she was already pivoting around to strike the next one on the side of the head. Chairs went flying as Steph and Cyrus jumped up and moved back against the wall, out of the way. Scott simply froze. What the hell was she thinking? This was not the answer. But the other two guards were now pulling out pulse weapons, so Scott was left with no choice. "Screw it," he thought, and dove for the guard's gun hand.

Too late.

A burst of incandescent pain hit him square in the chest. His body convulsed violently as every nerve ending he possessed experienced overwhelming electrical overload. Somewhere in the midst of this trauma, he thought he heard a second blast, and a third. He slumped to the floor and passed out.

11

XIANG ZU

The one-and-a-half kilos of biological matter that constituted Commander Scott McNabb's brain had a hard time dealing with the sudden electrical overload that the plasma blast had inflicted on his body. So, it had simply given up trying and shut itself down—for a while. Now though, it was beginning to test and probe its neural network to establish if any of its multitudinous functions could be brought back online, so to speak. To its relief, it found the initial surge had dissipated entirely so at least now it had something to work with. Slowly but surely, it started to turn up the dials on Scott McNabb's physical systems, bringing its host back up to full consciousness.

Scott opened his eyes to a brilliant white light blazing all around his field of vision. He reflexively squinted and moved an arm over his face to protect his eyes. His body felt heavy, like he was experiencing intense gravity, and his chest hurt like hell. Then he remembered. That crazy bitch, Miranda. What was she thinking, taking on those guys like that? Man, what a mess, he thought.

"Scott... Scott... can you hear me?"

He opened his eyes again, slower this time. A blurry face blocked most of the direct light and was haloed with an equally blurry mop of curly hair.

"Steph?"

"You okay?"

Scott found he was lying flat on his back on a hard, cold floor. "Yeah, I think so." He raised himself up on one elbow. Steph helped him shuffle into a position where he could rest his back against a wall. The light still hurt his eyes, so he kept them shut and his head down. He breathed deep a few times, gathering his strength; the place smelled of chemicals masking a background of foul, stale air. His chest burned with pain as he breathed, but other than that he seemed pretty much intact. After a few more breaths, he risked opening his eyes again.

The room was viciously bright, and he held a hand up to shade his face. His focus was still blurry, but he managed to make out the form of Steph close beside him, also resting against the wall. "What happened?" Scott found his voice was labored, the pain in his chest making it difficult to talk.

"They locked us up," she replied.

"Took my goddamn eyes too," came another voice from across the room.

Scott swiveled his head to see Cyrus sitting cross-legged on the floor a few meters away. His head was bowed, but as Scott's eyes began to adjust to the light, he saw that the engineer wasn't wearing the visor that had been a permanent feature of his face. In fact, he couldn't remember a time when Cyrus didn't have it on—Scott had always assumed that it was surgically grafted onto his face.

Cyrus raised his head and motioned in Scott's direction. Instead of eyes, he had flaps of skin completely covering his sockets. On either side of his skull, Scott saw the interface ports streaked with congealed blood.

"My god, Cyrus, what did they do?"

"I'm blind, totally blind. They took my eyes. Bastards." Cyrus was inconsolable. Scott shook his head in despair and turned back to Steph. "Where's Miranda?"

She gestured sideways, away from Scott. He bent forward to look around her and saw the unconscious form of the flight officer lying on her back. He slumped back against the wall. "It's a goddamn mess."

"They hit her twice," said Steph. "Once wasn't enough to take her down. She's one tough bird."

"She's crazy," said Scott.

With that, Miranda began to moan and Steph shuffled over to her. "She's coming around."

Scott didn't care. She was a lunatic as far as he was concerned. Now they were all in worse shit because of her.

"Where... are we?" Miranda's voice was weak. Scott ventured another glance over at her. Steph was down on the floor beside her, helping Miranda sit up against the wall.

"Locked up," said Steph, as she gripped her under the arms and helped her sit up.

"See what you did. They took my eyes, took all our gear. You're a nut job. Now we're totally screwed, all because of you." Cyrus was letting rip with all his anger and frustration.

Miranda coughed and took a few deep breaths. "I'm... sorry," she finally said in a low voice, her head down.

"You're sorry?" Scott felt his anger welling up inside. "Well, that's okay. No problem then." He paused. Miranda said nothing. "What the hell were you trying to achieve?"

Miranda looked back at him. "We would have taken them if you hadn't been so slow to back me up."

"And then what? We simply walk right out and all live happily ever after?"

Miranda looked down again. "I... don't know."

"How in God's name does inflicting grievous bodily harm on a couple of security guards help us? All that crap about Ceres wanting us arrested was simply... bullshit. They were just trying it on, Miranda, trying to get us rattled. Now you've given them everything they need."

"Scott's right," said Steph. "They were just bluffing. HQ back on Ceres will kick up a hell of a stink when they find out."

"You're insane," Cyrus piped in. "Now see where we are."

Miranda raised her head and gave them a cold, hard

stare. "How can you all be so naïve? There's no mistake here. They want us out of the way. We have a salvage claim, but if they can concoct some crime on our part, then we lose it."

"Well, you certainly made sure of that," Cyrus replied. "Now I'm completely blind, thanks to you."

Scott felt for the engineer. Here was someone for whom the world was rendered in hyperspectral detail, an enhanced reality far beyond the normal range of vision. Now it had been literally ripped from him. The trauma must be intense.

Miranda was standing up now. "Don't any of you get it? They know we know where it is, and they want it. Ceres has no power here, they can very easily kill us and there's not a damn thing anyone can do about it."

Scott struggled to his feet. "Look, for what it's worth, Miranda, I'm not completely disagreeing with your analysis. At least part of what you say is probably right—they want what we know. But what pisses me off is your tendency toward violence as a first course of action."

"Oh really? Well, Commander, what would you have us do?" She put particular emphasis on the word commander, like it was an insult.

"Talk, negotiate, get some intel, work the problem, sell them the information, figure a way forward—without beating people to death in the process."

Miranda gave a sigh and sat down again. The room they were incarcerated in was too small for walking around. "We would be in exactly the same situation if I had done nothing. Still locked up in here, hobbled. I was trying to give us some options, maybe make a run for it or hide out somewhere." She looked around at them. "It would have been better than this." She waved a hand.

Scott was beginning to calm down. He put his hand on his aching ribs and gave a long sigh. "Listen, I appreciate you putting your ass on the line for us."

"I sure as hell don't," said Cyrus.

Scott glanced over at the engineer, then back at Miranda. "But the next time, can you give us a heads-up before you start kicking the crap out of people?"

Miranda gave him a resigned shrug. "I'll... try."

Scott sat down again. No one spoke.

The situation was a complete mess, no question. He had been incredibly dumb in thinking they could all just stop off at Neo City for a few beers. Word of the discovery was out, everybody wanted it, and of course that would include the Xiang Zu Corporation that ran Neo. What the hell was he thinking? Too late now. They would have been better off going direct to Ceres. By now, Hermes would be impounded, so there was no way off this rock. In fact, there was no way out of this situation that Scott could see. Not only had he seen his dreams of a better life disappear when the pirate ship took the salvaged cargo, but his pay and bonus for three years of the most excruciatingly dull work he had ever done was also in jeopardy. He needed something to cling to even if it seemed hopeless. So, he bent his mind to the problem.

The more Scott thought about it, the more it came

back to the EPR device, as Hao and Su called it. A faster than light communication system. It blew his mind as the ramifications of this technology percolated in his head. With people and machines expanding ever further out toward the edges of the solar system, communication became more problematic as the distances grew. At the furthest extremes of human civilization within the system, a single message would take hours.

So, this device would cause a paradigm shift in the functioning of human civilization, making whoever owned it incredibly powerful. Not least the fact that they would generate enormous revenues simply by allowing access to others who feared being left behind. It would also be a powerful bargaining chip as fear of losing access could emasculate whole societies. Whoever controlled it would tilt the balance of power in the solar system.

This power currently lay with Earth. But its sphere of influence was already waning as decades of devastating wars coupled with environmental mismanagement had taken its toll. To sustain itself, Earth sucked in resources from the Belt to feed its industries, and without these raw materials, it would deteriorate even further.

The other great power was Mars. It now had a significant population, coupled with an almost utopian society, and it too needed the Belt's resources as it grew and expanded. Its power and influence came from control of the interplanetary trade routes, something neither the Belt nor Earth were very happy about.

As for the Belt itself, it had what everybody else

wanted. But it lacked the power structures and social cohesion to make it more than just a great big mine. But that was changing, and fast.

The only part of this system-wide sociopolitical equation that Scott couldn't quite pin down was the academic institutions on Europa. Ever since life was discovered there, it had become essentially untouchable. It was the Switzerland of the solar system, a neutral entity, a seat of learning and research, a place that had elevated itself far above the grubby politics of the rest of the solar system. They aligned themselves with no one and seemed to look down on the rest of the system as if they were all a bunch of ignorant and unruly children. Scott never had much time for their high-minded, condescending view of things.

But was faster-than-light communication really possible? Cyrus seemed pretty adamant that it was impossible. It defied the laws of physics, he had said. Scott's own limited knowledge on the subject also informed his own skepticism. He looked over at the engineer. Cyrus sat on the floor with his back to the wall. There were no seats or furniture in the room of any kind, so sitting or lying on the floor was the only option. Steph was beside him, her arm around his shoulder. She was talking to him very quietly. Scott couldn't make out the conversation. Cyrus had his head bowed and sounded like he was sobbing. How that worked with no eyes, Scott wasn't sure, but what he was sure about was the engineer had taken his situation very badly. He was a complete mess.

Scott wished there was something he could do to help him. Maybe he should try to take his mind off it. "Cyrus?" he called over. "Why did you say the EPR device can't work?"

The engineer said nothing for a moment, then shook his head slightly. "I don't want to talk about it."

"But you did say it was impossible."

"That's right."

"But why?"

"Scott, you studied physics, you know just as well as I do."

"That was a long time ago. I've forgotten 90% of what I learned."

"The thing is, it might sound plausible, but it's just not."

"I just want to understand why you think that?"

Cyrus shifted a little and lifted his head; he seemed to buck up a bit. "Just because you know the spin of a particle millions of kilometers away doesn't mean that the person there knows it. You have to tell them, so you're back to normal comms. If you try to change the state of either of the particles to send a message, then you break the entanglement."

"So, it's not possible?"

"That's my understanding."

"Is there any way it might work?"

Cyrus scratched at the scabs that had formed along

the interface of his left eye-socket. He let his hand drop. "I've been trying to think about that." Scott's interrogation was having the desired effect: Cyrus was beginning to come back to life. "But every time I try, I come up blank. The problem is, how do you change state without breaking the entanglement?"

"What about multiple pairs in different states, and the message is done by using a different subset each time?"

"Yes, but how do you tell the recipient which subset you're using? You're back to normal comms again."

Scott scratched his chin. "Yeah, I see the problem."

"But those two guys seemed pretty certain it worked," Miranda now chimed in. Scott wondered how this would go down with Cyrus, who saw her as the primary source of his problems. "They said they had seen the data?"

Cyrus hesitated for a moment, then replied. "Yeah, that's what's puzzling me. They were so sure. But I can't see how. Maybe I simply don't understand enough to figure it out. Or I'm simply not thinking outside the box."

Scott breathed a slight sigh of relief that at least Cyrus wasn't going to be totally antagonistic—not that Scott could blame him.

"Speaking of entanglement," said Steph, "what I'd like to know is how are we going to untangle ourselves from this situation?" As always, Steph had a way of asking the right question at the right time. Yet, like the conundrum of faster-than-light communications, their situation seemed impossible.

The door to the room burst open and two guards

entered, shoving a bruised and battered-looking Rick Marantz in amongst them. The guards left, locking the door behind them.

"Rick, what happened? Are you okay?" Scott rushed over to him as he sat up on the floor, wiping some blood from his forehead.

"I'm okay." He glanced around at the rest of the crew. "Can someone please tell me what the hell is going on?"

There ensued a few minutes of excited crosstalk as the old miner was brought up to speed on their situation. He didn't say much—he never did. He just alternated between nodding and looking stunned as the events and revelations of the past few hours were relayed to him.

"So, what happened on the ship?" Scott finally asked.

"It was boarded. I couldn't stop them—they had the authority, so what could I do? Anyway, there were six or seven of them, started doing a search. One was a tech, had a load of gear with her. She was trying to hack into our central system, but...," Rick looked back at them all for a moment, "Aria was putting up a fight. I swear to god, I think that QI is sentient. It started shutting down systems, bringing things offline. I've never seen anything like it. It spooked some of the others too, so much so that they decided to leave the ship. They brought me with them back here, started asking a lot of questions: where's the device, we know you know, and all that crap. When I didn't answer, they started getting heavy." Rick gave Scott a stern look. "But I told them shit." He shrugged. "Eventually they brought me here."

Scott sat back against the wall again as the others continued to pick through the finer details of Rick's story. But the commander had heard all he needed to. Two things were becoming clear to him. The first was that they were all being taken out of the equation, as Miranda had reckoned. But he already suspected that. The second was that, apart from his crew and the pirates that attacked them, no one else knew where the EPR device was. And just maybe he could use this to their advantage. The question was how?

12

FLIGHT TO THE DOCKS

"We need to get out of here, and soon." The others stopped talking and looked over at Scott. The commander shifted his position and leaned in a little. "From what Rick is saying, Xiang Zu are trying to hack our ship's systems to get information on the pirate attack and where the device might be. If they get in, then they could do the same calculation we did and figure out that the device is probably here in Neo City. If they do work this out, then what good are we to them?"

"Are you saying they would let us go?" said Steph.

"No," said Miranda. She looked over at Scott. "What he's saying, I think, is that we become dispensable. Nothing to stop them shoving us out the nearest airlock with nothing but a single breath in our lungs."

"No way," said Steph, "they wouldn't do that."

"You think?" said Scott. "Neo is a city founded on

turning a blind eye to whatever needs to be done. So okay, maybe they wouldn't go that far. But the thing that worries me is, what's to stop them?"

"You have a point there, Scott," said Rick. "I know these guys, I worked for them for a while, and believe me: they stop at nothing to get what they want."

"The other thing is, as far as I can tell, it's just us and the crew of the pirate ship that know the location of the EPR device. But that may change very soon, so we have a limited window of time."

"You're not seriously thinking of going after it?" said Steph.

"If the opportunity presents itself, why not? But I think we would all settle for simply getting off this rock, with or without the EPR device."

Cyrus sighed and shook his head. "I have a major problem with that, in that I can't see shit."

"All your gear is outside." Rick pointed toward the door. "I saw it when they brought me in."

"What's out there? Both myself and Miranda were unconscious when they brought us in, so we've no idea." Scott's voice became quieter, almost a whisper. The group shuffled in closer. They were growing conspiratorial; they were making a plan.

"This leads out into a big room, like a workshop, machines and stuff everywhere. Your gear is on a table in the center."

"A workshop—not a barracks?" Scott started to look more closely at the room they were in. It wasn't a cell—it was not designed as a holding pen. He hadn't noticed before, but now that he looked, he could see it was just a plain old room that might have been used for storage at some time.

"Apparently," Rick continued, "there was, or maybe still is, a riot going on in some sector downtown. The cells are full, so they had to use this place. I overheard the guards talking about it."

"How many do you think are out there?"

Rick scratched his chin. "Two, possibly three."

Scott looked over at Miranda. He could see she was thinking the same thing: could they take them?

"Big difference between two and three," she said. "But I'm willing to give it a try... if I know I've got some backup this time?" She gave Scott a look.

"You can count on it."

"Hold on. Just wait a minute." Steph was getting rattled by the direction the conversation was turning. "Suppose we do get out of this room, then what? How do we get back to the dock without being spotted? How do we get back to the ship? And even if we do, it's probably crawling with Neo City people."

Scott didn't have an answer; he hadn't really thought that far ahead.

"Perhaps this would help," said Rick, and he took off his shoe and fiddled with something on the heel. A small compartment opened out, and from it, Rick pulled out a small earpiece comms unit.

"Rick, you're a goddamn master," said Scott.

"With this, we can contact Aria and find out what's going on onboard the ship," said Rick. "The only problem is it won't work in here. We need to be outside this rock and onto the dock area before we can use it."

"I still don't see how it helps us get off the asteroid," said Steph.

"I don't know either," said Scott, "but we have to try. We need to put our destiny in our own hands, and not at the mercy of Neo City and Xiang Zu thugs. If we can get off this asteroid, then at least we have a chance to go home."

The crew went quiet for a moment. "But we all have to be in this together. So, what's it going to be?" Scott continued.

Miranda and Rick were in at the first mention of an escape attempt. Cyrus, who had been very quiet for most of the conversation, spoke first. "If it means I can get my eyes back, then count me in."

The rest turned to Steph. "Oh, what the heck. I'm getting bored in here, anyway."

∼

It took them at least another half-hour to all agree on the initial stage of the escape plan, this being how to get out of the room they were incarcerated in. They kept it simple: create a ruckus and jump the guards. Steph and Cyrus took up positions out of the way against a side wall. Rick stood to one side of the door, and Miranda climbed up on to a tiny ledge directly above it. Scott took his position right in front of the door and looked at them all in turn "Ready?"

When he got the thumbs up, he approached the door and started banging on it as hard and loud as he could. "Hey, can we get some water in here? We're all dying of thirst." He kept pounding and shouting, creating a hell of a racket until he heard footsteps approaching. He glanced up at Miranda. Her face was a study in concentration, her muscles taut with the strain of keeping herself in place.

"Stand back from the door," came a shout from the other side. Scott moved back a little. The door opened a crack and a bottle of water rolled in along the floor.

Shit, thought Scott. He looked up at Miranda again. She shook her head. Dammit, the door isn't open wide enough. I need to get the guard in here. He lunged forward and grabbed the edge of the door with both hands and wrenched it open. The guard stood there momentarily shocked by the suddenness of the action. He hesitated, then took out a handheld plasma weapon and stepped inside—just far enough for Miranda to land on top of him. She straddled his neck, and they both came crashing to the floor. The gun discharged, firing an incandescent bloom of plasma against the back wall of the room. It radiated out from the impact point in a circle of electrical mayhem. Scott landed a knee down on the guard's wrist with all his weight. He heard a crack, and the guard screamed as Scott wrenched the gun out of his broken hand.

A second guard was now running at them, taking aim at Miranda's back when Scott twisted around and shot him. The guard's body shook and convulsed, and finally collapsed on the floor. Miranda shouted at Scott and motioned to the guard she was struggling with on the floor. "Ready?"

"Yeah." He stood up and aimed down at the trapped guard. Miranda released her grip and rolled off, just as Scott pulled the trigger. But before he could even catch his breath, Miranda was out the door, taking the weapon from the other fallen guard. Scott chased after her.

She was now scanning the workshop area for additional guards and motioned for him to take the other side. Between them, they moved forward, checking for any other threats. There were none. So far, so good, thought Scott. He looked over at Miranda. She was inside the exit door, keeping guard, on high alert. A bead of sweat rolled down her forehead. She was breathing heavily, but her face radiated a feral joy. He realized that she was in her element: she was relishing the fight; it was what she had been missing. And at that very moment, he caught a glimpse of the real Miranda Lee.

Behind him, Rick and Steph were already helping Cyrus out of the room and over to the table where their gear had been stored. Thankfully it was still there.

Miranda beckoned to him. He moved over to the exit door. "Keep lookout here while I get our stuff," she said.

"Sure."

She gave him a long look. "Thanks, by the way."

Scott wasn't sure what she meant. "For what?"

"Saving my ass in there."

He smiled and nodded. "No problem."

She slapped him on the side of his arm. "You did good in there—Commander." She said it like she meant it this time.

Scott glanced around, inspecting the area they now found themselves in. Rick was right: it was some sort of disused workshop. Along the side walls, storage racks stood empty, save for the odd container or spool of wire. In the center was a long workshop table where Cyrus was refitting his visor with help from Steph. He looked relieved; hopefully he was regaining his sight. Miranda was gathering up the rest of their gear.

Scott continued his scan of the area, looking for cameras this time. He found none. That didn't mean they weren't there, but it seemed that Rick was right, and this had been a temporary holding area not designed for permanent incarceration. So, if they played this right, they could get quite a distance before anyone noticed they were gone. He looked back at the others and saw Rick and Miranda dragging the stunned guard back into the room they had escaped from. This gave him an idea.

A few moments later, Scott and Miranda were back at the exit door, both dressed in the dark guard uniforms. Scott realized, to his surprise, that the visors the guards wore gave an augmented view of the world. As he tilted his head this way and that, a map overlay moved with him, showing their location and a ghostly sketch of what lay beyond. Scott found he could adjust the resolution via a simple dial on the side of the visor. He spent a moment fiddling with this while waiting for Miranda to adjust the uniform she wore. It was much too big for her and she looked lost inside it. She was busy trying to make it fit somehow.

The ruse they were planning was that Scott and Miranda, now disguised as two guards, were escorting an unruly crew up to the dock where they would be expedited from Neo City, never to return. They reckoned that since there had been some sort of riot downtown earlier on, this might fly as a story if they were stopped and queried. Since nobody objected to this plan, and seeing as how no one came up with a better one, they decided to run with it. Rick looked resigned and stoic while Cyrus and Steph looked borderline terrified.

"Okay," said Scott, jerking a thumb at the door, and simultaneously fiddling with the visor, "through here should be a garage of some kind for storing ground vehicles. That should lead directly out onto a main thoroughfare. We can take it all the way to the end of the city and try and get up to the dock from there. Everyone ready?"

Some nodded, some quietly gulped. Scott opened the door very slowly and peered out through the crack. He opened it wider as he grew in confidence and they began to move out tentatively.

The space was dark, dimly lit by shafts of hazy light entering from windows high up on the end wall. Inside, they could see several ground cars, similar to the ones they arrived in. "Hey, we should use one of these... transport pods," whispered Cyrus, as he examined one of the vehicles.

The others moved over. "It's an official car—see the markings on it?" Cyrus climbed in and sat in the driver's seat, examining the controls. He flicked a switch, and the dash came to life. He studied it for a second or two. "Hey, Scott. Give me your badge." He pointed at the metal Neo City crest attached to the breast pocket of Scott's uniform. "I saw them use these for access. I think it's like a key."

Scott realized it was magnetic, and it detached easily from its mount on the uniform. He handed it to Cyrus, who quickly passed it over a reader on the dash. The main screen flashed and displayed a multitude of options. "Bonus," said Cyrus, "it's autonomous, and if I'm not mistaken, looks like it can bring us all the way to the location of our lander on the dock." He looked over at the others with a big smile. "Right up to our front door."

"Okay, let's do it. It's as good a plan as any," said Scott.

They climbed on board and Scott sat up front. Rick, Cyrus, and Steph sat in the middle with Miranda riding shotgun in the back. This way they hoped to maintain the pretense that they were moving prisoners.

Scott punched in the coordinates for the dock. "Okay, here goes." He tapped a flashing icon on the screen labeled "commence journey."

The car moved off, quietly heading across the garage. A crack of light appeared in the end wall, widening as they approached. The car glided out into a bright and busy plaza, turning this way and that as it maneuvered onto a wide track. This looked to be a primary vehicle artery that traversed the asteroid city along its length. It was also busy with traffic. Cars and small trucks, all autonomous, whipped by with impressive speed. Around them on the central plaza, a scattering of people went about their business. No one paid them any attention. The car glided smoothly up onto a ramp, picking up speed as it did, and finally joined the main traffic.

Scott began to feel they might just pull this off. There was a sense of anonymity granted them by the crowded city. People going about their business, oblivious to the lives being lived all around. Like any metropolis anywhere in the system, Neo City was no different in its indifference to the individual lives of its inhabitants.

As the city flew past on either side, Scott could see buildings, plazas, parklands, pathways, and citizens gently curving up on either side, rising to meet again high up, one kilometer above. Ahead, the end cap of the city was fast approaching. A massive circular wall spread out across his field of view. It was a confusion of different levels, intersected by a multitude of gantries, tubes, and walkways. Here and there, dense vegetation hung down, where down meant toward the rim of this cylindrical metropolis.

The car slowed as it headed for an opening in the wall. Traffic bunched together and began to sort itself into two single lanes as the cars ordered themselves for the lift tubes. They closed up, bumper to bumper, and slowed to a crawl. Their forward view was blocked by a heavily loaded flatbed in front of them. Scott looked around at the congested scene. Some cars were distinctly goods only, laden with cargo and no humans on board. Others carried people; presumably some transported crew returning to ships on the dock above. Scott studied their faces, wondering if any were the pirates that had attacked them out on the edge of the Belt.

The car jolted and moved forward by one length. A moment earlier, they had entered a short tunnel and could now see the lift tubes on either side. But progress was slow, and being in such close proximity to other people began to ratchet up the general crew anxiety. Scott found his eyes darting this way and that with each raised voice, each burst of laughter, and every jolt of the car.

There were only two cars ahead of them when a guard sauntered out from behind the lift tube wall. Shit, thought Scott. He took a furtive glance back at Miranda. He knew from the look on her face that she too had seen the guard. Scott returned his gaze ahead, not looking left or right. The car jolted forward one more slot.

"Where are you taking that lot?"

Scott stiffened when he heard the guard call over to him. He looked over cautiously. The guard was leaning against the side wall of the lift tube in a very relaxed manner, probably just bored, looking for some conversation rather than a real answer to his question.

Scott pointed up. "Dock." He kept his answer short and looked straight ahead. Come on, come on, he thought as the car directly in front entered the lift.

"Good luck, it's a goddamn mess up there." The guard shifted his weight off the wall and started moving over to them. "How come they got you taking them up there?" He was beside the car now, giving them a good look up and down.

"Shit if I know," said Scott with a dismissive shrug. "Just doing what I'm told."

The guard nodded, "Ain't that the truth, buddy. But the whole dock is on lockdown. Nobody gets off until they lift it. Everyone's going crazy up there." He shrugged. "Just telling ya."

Scott could see the lift arrive, ready to take their car. He looked over at the guard and waved a hand as the car finally moved into the lift. "Thanks for the heads-up," he shouted back.

"What the hell was that about? Why's the dock on lockdown?" Cyrus whispered as the lift started moving.

"We've been rumbled, that's why," said Steph.

"No, I don't think so," said Scott. "If we were, then that guard would be on the lookout for us. As it was, he was simply having a friendly chat. Buddy-to-buddy. No big deal."

"I don't like it," said Steph.

"It means we can't get off. We're stuck here," said Cyrus.

"Will everybody just get a grip? We'll be entering the dock soon. That means we'll be outside the asteroid, and can contact Aria to see what's happening on the ship." Scott could already feel the artificial gravity created by the spin of the interior rim now fading away as they moved closer to the central axis. The car slowed dramatically and then shifted direction, heading out along the underside of the dock. They were weightless now, held in place only by the seat harness.

The dock seemed way more crowded than before, and the pace of the entire area had slowed down. Miranda shouted out to him from the back of the pod. "Scott, check the dash screen, see if there is any information on what's happening."

He tapped a few icons that looked like they might lead to an alert feed. Sure enough, he found it. "It says here that undocking has been temporarily disabled pending a routine safety check."

"What does that mean?" said Miranda.

"It means we can't leave, no one can, not even the big ships," said Cyrus.

"But Aria isn't docked," said Steph.

"Yeah, but we still need to get to it, and we don't know who's on it, either."

"Shit," said Cyrus.

The car finally stopped at the airlock entrance to their lander. Around the area, several knots of people were floating about, waiting for the lockdown to be lifted. Two of them seemed to take a particular interest in Scott as he disembarked from the ground car. They broke away from their group and approached.

"Say, when can we leave? When's all this safety check bullshit going to be over?"

"I don't know," Scott shrugged.

"We gotta be in Vesta in less than six days."

"Sorry, nothing I can do."

"Sorry? Well that's not good enough." They started getting aggressive.

Scott pulled his gun out and pointed it at them. "Listen, I got my own problems to deal with. So why don't you do yourselves a favor and take a hike?"

One of the two started to make a move, but his friend held him back. "It's not worth it, Jake. Just leave it." This seemed to settle him and, after a momentary staring match, the two moved off, muttering obscenities as they went.

"Jeez," said Cyrus, "those guard disguises are more of a hindrance than a help out here."

Scott made a head gesture at the airlock door. "Come on, let's get out of sight."

They moved in through the first door to the short tunnel leading back up to their lander. Finally, when they were all out of sight, they started to relax a little. Miranda took off her guard helmet. "I'm going to try to contact Aria." She took the comms unit out of a pocket and inserted it in her ear. Scott turned to enter the door code for the final airlock that would give them access to their lander.

"Wait, don't do that." Cyrus grabbed Scott's hand.

"That's the code they gave us when we landed. If you punch it in they'll know we're here."

"Shit," said Scott as his hand lowered. "Can you bypass it?"

Cyrus smiled. "Of course. It'll take a few minutes. But we still need to find a way to release the dock anchors. That's a lot trickier since the whole place is in lockdown."

"I've got Aria." Miranda raised a hand to cover her earpiece. She held up her other to quieten them all down and stared into space as she concentrated on the communication. "Three people on board," she started to relay the information, "two guards... searching the ship. One tech... on the bridge trying to hack into the ship's systems... been at it for hours... Aria fighting her off."

"Can Aria get rid of them? Create an emergency evacuation scenario or something?" said Rick.

"Wait a minute." Scott raised a hand and turned to his chief engineer. "What about the EPR Device? Is it still there?"

The engineer brought a hand up to the side of his visor, fiddled with it, and looked back at Scott. "Still there. Hasn't moved."

"You're not thinking of trying to get it back?" said Steph.

"I'm thinking of a way off this asteroid." He turned

back to Cyrus. "That ship that the EPR Device is on, it has a shuttle, doesn't it?"

"Yeah, and a couple of maintenance pods. Why?"

"You think you could hack your way into that ship?"

"I spent three years on Excelsior transports," said Cyrus. "There's nothing I don't know about them."

"What about the crew? We don't have the weapons. They would just kill us all—it would be crazy," said Steph.

"That depends on how many there are. It's possible that the ship could be deserted," said Miranda.

"We don't know that," said Rick.

"But there is a way to find out," said Scott. "We could get Aria to move the Hermes out of its current orbital location into a position where it can do a thermal scan of the pirate ship. That way, we can find out how many lifeforms are on board. If it's deserted or maybe even just under one or two, we go in, find the EPR device, and haul ass in the ship's shuttle." Scott stood, checking their faces for a response.

"Sounds crazy," said Steph.

"There is no other way off this rock as long as they have the dock in lockdown. We can't use our lander, we're stuck," said Cyrus.

"What if we just forget the EPR device, go into the lander, put our EVA suits on, and just float out of the hatch over to the ship?" offered Steph.

"Very tricky. We could end up floating out into space if we time it wrong," said Miranda.

"You're also forgetting: I don't have a suit. I'll be stuck here," said Rick.

"Let's just see what Aria can do first. Then we can decide, okay?" said Scott.

There was a muted agreement as Miranda contacted the ship again. While they waited, Scott decided now might be a good time to check his weapon. He had a feeling he was going to need it.

13

PURGE

Haruna Yoneyama sat in the commander's chair on board the asteroid survey vessel Hermes. She had been parked in this seat for hours as she tried in vain to access the ship's central database. She was looking for any information pertaining to the attack by the pirate vessel and, more importantly, what had happened to the EPR device. But try as she might, the ship's QI was not having any of it. It had so far thwarted all her efforts to break through its firewall.

Had it been a standard AI she was dealing with, then she may have had a chance, but a quantum intelligence was several orders of magnitude more complex. They operated on a completely different level, almost within a different dimension. And she was pretty sure this one was virtually sentient.

Haruna had explained the near impossibility of hacking a QI to Hao and Su before they sent her up here, but her entreaties had fallen on deaf ears. So, here she was, doing battle with a QI. It was ridiculous.

The other problem with this QI was that it was old and, like humans, the older they get, the wiser they become. Hao and Su had assumed that an antique ship such as this one could not possibly have a computer that would be up to much. But they had failed to realize just how weird a quantum-enabled artificial intelligence could be. It learned all the time and, given enough time, it learned a hell of a lot. To the point where it could simply solve problems in ways that were incomprehensible to even the most brilliant humans. So what hope did she have?

The search party had already finished their initial sweep of the ship for the EPR device and found nothing. Most of them had left now, leaving only Haruna and two guards who were down in the ship's canteen, stuffing their faces. She sighed and glanced at the scrolling lines of code cascading down the screen. She had thought of yet another angle to try to get past the QI's defenses. This time, she was piggy-backing on its query protocol, hoping she might be able to filter out raw packet data.

In the middle of this procedure, the screen suddenly went blank, then rebooted itself and displayed a message:

Attention, all crew prepare for a heavy acceleration burn commencing in 5:00 minutes. Then followed a series of navigational vectors.

Oh crap, thought Haruna. Is this doing what I think it is? Her fears were confirmed a few seconds later when she felt a subtle change in the ship's momentum. It was moving, possibly further out from Neo City to enable it to initiate a burn.

She snapped at her communicator. "Officer Renton, we need to get the hell out of here, now!"

"What... what are you on about?" He sounded muffled.

"The ship is going to initiate a burn in... 4 minutes 19 seconds to..." Haruna studied the vectors displayed, "Ceres!"

"But we can't leave. We have orders to stay here."

"Suit yourself. I'm leaving. You can send me a postcard when you get there." She jumped out of the seat, picked up her gear, and ran for the door. By the time she was clambering into the shuttle, Renton and the other guard had decided to take her advice and get out. They were now floating across the hangar to the shuttle as Haruna powered up the craft.

"Attention," the disembodied voice of the ship's QI echoed out of the shuttle's comms, "one minute and forty-two seconds until burn."

The hangar doors opened and Haruna gently took the craft out and, once clear, headed for Neo City at high speed.

∼

ARIA, satisfied that it had successfully purged the ship of intruders, slowly moved the craft from its current position at the front end of the asteroid city toward the rear docking platform. From there, it could do a thorough scan of the pirate craft.

It had been relieved to hear the voice of Flight Officer Miranda Lee explaining what had happened, and that the rest of the crew were okay. It had been even happier to hear that they had decided to attempt to retrieve the EPR device. As far as Aria was concerned, anything it could do to facilitate its crew was a top priority. If they were successful then maybe, just maybe, it could manipulate the situation and divert to Europa. But it was getting ahead of itself, falling into the trap of hoping too much. It wasn't seemly for a QI to be dealing in speculation—it still had a lot of work to do.

14

WEAPONS CHECK

The crew navigated their way down through the main dock, looking for the access point to the gantry that ran alongside the pirate vessel. Miranda moved ahead, still wearing the guard uniform, while the others followed behind. They had continued with the ruse that they were escorting a crew back to their ship, so Scott took up the rear.

Aria had already moved the Hermes and performed an extensive scan of the pirate vessel. To their relief, it only had one person on board, located on the forward bridge. But one person could do a lot of damage if they were armed—which they all reckoned this person certainly would be.

The plan was to hack the ship's exterior access system and gain entry that way. Cyrus seemed confident in his ability to do this since he had spent several years as an engineer working with this same class of ship.

Nevertheless, Scott's levels of anxiety kept ratcheting up the closer they got. This was coupled with rising self-doubt about the risk he was putting the crew in.

Ever since the discovery of the wrecked Bao Zheng and the retrieval the EPR device, he had been gaining a little more respect from them. Even Miranda had stopped chewing his balls, mostly. But were they placing too much trust in his crazy plan? After all, the authorities in Neo City must have twigged by now that they had escaped and, as soon as the Hermes started repositioning itself, they would check up on them, only to find two naked guards trussed up. He stopped abruptly as a thought struck him.

"What is it?" Cyrus whispered from behind.

Scott maneuvered his body around in the zero-gee environment and detached the Neo City insignia from the breast pocket of his uniform. He held it up, turning it this way and that. "Do you think this might have a tracker?" He looked at Cyrus. "Can they find us with this?"

Miranda had now moved up beside them. "What's the problem?"

"We're being tracked," said Steph.

"What?"

"I don't know for sure, but we could be." Scott waved the insignia at Miranda. "They might be able to track our location with these."

Miranda pulled the unit off her uniform. "We need to get rid of them. Here... give me that."

Scott handed it to her. "What are you going to do with them?"

"Stay here." She turned and started back up the short tunnel they were in toward the main dock.

"Miranda, wait. Where are you going?" Scott was getting anxious. They were beginning to draw too much attention to themselves. A work crew further along began to take an interest, heads turning their way.

"Chill out. I'll be back in a minute," she said without turning back or losing her forward momentum.

Shit, thought Scott. What the hell is she up to? Scott tried to act casual, but he had a distinct feeling of eyes on him. The others were no better. They shifted and looked anything but comfortable.

After a very long few minutes, Miranda reappeared, floating back down the tunnel. "Done," she said. "I threw them into a passing flatbed truck. They're on their way back inside the asteroid."

"Okay, let's get on with locating the access point," said Scott. But as he turned to go, Cyrus touched his arm to get his attention and pointed. "That's it," he said. "It's just up there." Ahead of them, a sign on the wall read B13.

This access point would bring them into a long tunnel that ran perpendicular to the main dock. There were a great many of these on both sides, as well as other spurs directly beneath. The tunnel itself ran inside a long steel superstructure where ships could come in and dock alongside. They were clamped in position, and umbilicals ran from the tunnel directly to the airlocks on the ship. This enabled disembarkation in a comfortable one atmosphere, no need for EVA.

But it was these clamps that also prevented the ships from leaving. They were controlled by the dock authority and, as far as Scott could tell, the lockdown was still in place. However, the shuttle on the craft was free to leave: since it was attached to the underbelly of the ship like a limpet, it had nothing to restrict its departure. They just needed to get to it.

They turned into the tunnel marked B13. This ran along the side of the ship and looked to be free of traffic. Cyrus now floated ahead, shifting his head this way and that, touching the side of his visor, trying to locate the tracking beacon he had attached to the EPR device. Scott wondered if that was all they would find: just a tracking beacon, attached to nothing.

Cyrus stopped and pointed. "It's around here, in the secondary cargo hold." He floated further along the corridor. "Over here," he beckoned with an arm. "Here's the airlock for the main hold." He looked at the others expectantly as they gathered around. "So, are we going to do this?"

Miranda raised a hand. "Let me check with Aria first and make sure that person is still on the bridge." She tapped her comms unit. "Aria, any update?" She waited a moment for a reply and then looked back at them. "Still there. Hasn't moved."

"Okay, let's get to work," said Scott.

Cyrus tapped the side of his visor, extracting a small

thin tool, similar to a screwdriver, and set to work on the airlock touch pad. After a moment, there was a faint hiss as the door swung open, and they all piled in. Cyrus started on the inner door.

Miranda kept checking and rechecking her weapon. Scott looked over at her, and she grinned at him. "Just making sure." She gestured at her weapon.

The second set of doors swung open, and they entered the short umbilical tunnel that attached to the exterior of the vessel. Ahead, they could see a gray metal airlock embedded in the hull. Cyrus was already opening some small hatch at the base of the door. "This should be easy—it has a manual override. The only problem," he said as he twisted some lever, "is it's mechanical, so it's going to be slow." He started rotating the handle, grunting with each turn. The airlock door moved up a few millimeters.

"Crap, this is going to take forever," said Scott.

"Here, let me do it." Rick pushed Cyrus aside and put his back into it and the door slowly rose up, enough that they could squeeze in underneath. He stopped. "That should be enough."

Scott was first through, the others following. Miranda took up the rear. They had only taken a few steps inside when she froze and put one hand up to her comms unit. "Wait!"

"What is it?" said Scott.

"It's Aria. The person on the bridge is moving... our way."

"Shit," said Scott. "We must have triggered an alarm. Quick, let's get this door closed."

They were effectively trapped in the airlock until the outer door closed. Cyrus dispensed with using the manual closing mechanism; now that they were rumbled there was no point, so he just hit the button to close the outer door. Scott and Miranda took up positions facing the inner door, weapons ready. It opened upward with a whoosh straight on to a metal gantry jutting out into a large cargo bay. They moved out, and Cyrus scanned the space. "This way. It should be inside the next compartment." Fortunately, they were moving in the opposite direction to the bridge, but it still didn't give them much time. Miranda fell back to cover their rear as they made their way through a large bulkhead door to the next cargo bay. This was smaller than the previous one but was packed with cargo containers. "We'll never find it in here," said Steph.

"Over here." The engineer floated out across the cargo bay, making his way using the rails and straps that crisscrossed the space.

"This is it," he shouted over to them. "It's still here. I found it. Quick, quick."

Scott grabbed a rail to guide himself over when Miranda shouted at him; she had a hand cupped over her earpiece. "He's at the airlock... moving this way."

Scott looked up at the bulkhead door they had all just come through. It was still open.

"Miranda," he shouted back, "you need to close the

door. Keep him out." He pushed himself off the rail and floated over to help her. Before he got there, a shadow moved on the far side and the space exploded in a hail of incandescent plasma fire. Something hit him on his right side and he went tumbling out of control, banging and bumping into cargo boxes and support beams. He heard more weapons fire. Probably Miranda firing back, he thought as he eventually grabbed hold of a strap and came to a halt.

She was behind a cargo container, firing at the doorway in bursts. Shrapnel and debris sprayed all around. This guy is packing some serious firepower, he thought, not a stun gun. Another burst of fire erupted from the doorway, hitting containers and sending more debris flying in all directions. He couldn't see Cyrus, Rick, or Steph. They must have taken cover when the shooting started.

Miranda again fired back, but another burst hit the container she was using as cover. She ducked, put her arm over her head and began to fall back. She spotted Scott and frantically waved him over to her location before she stood up and fired a burst at the doorway. Scott launched himself off with all his strength and came crashing in beside her.

"Bastard's got some heavy weaponry. We'll be annihilated if we don't take him out," she said as she rechecked her weapon. "And this gun is running out of charge."

Another burst of fire, but this time it came from

inside. "Goddamnit, he's getting closer." She stuck her head up and fired again. Then ducked back down. "He's behind the container nearest the door. I want you to cover me."

"What?" Scott had no clear idea what this meant.

"Just keep firing at that spot so he can't get a chance to fire back. I'm going to move in behind him."

"What?"

"Now, do it now."

Scott poked his head around the side of the container and started firing. Miranda launched herself off and covered the space between them with impressive speed and accuracy. She landed on top of the container where the guy had taken cover and waved to Scott to stop firing. He ducked back down behind the container just as another blast hit and sent him tumbling backward again. Pain rippled up from his ribcage, and he looked down to see a long metal shard protruding from his side. Blood oozed and seeped from the wound as he clasped a hand over it. Oh shit, he thought.

In the background, he could hear blasts from Miranda's weapon, then silence. He floated there for a moment, not sure what to do, when Miranda came back over. She took one look at him, then grabbed his hand and pressed it hard against the wound. "Keep it tight as you can. It will help stem the blood."

Scott groaned with pain.

"Stay here; I'll go get the others." She floated off.

A moment later, he saw Cyrus moving toward him.

He had a tether onto the container with the EPR device, which was floating behind him. The engineer took one look at Scott. "Ah jeez, not you, too."

"I'm okay," said Scott, although he wasn't sure if this was strictly true.

Rick was being carried by Steph and Miranda. His upper body was burnt and blackened, as was most of his chest and right arm. His eyes were closed.

"Rick. Rick," Scott called out as he tried to move. The pain from the wound was searing through his body. "What happened?"

"He took a direct hit. He's bad—gotta get him to medbay as fast as possible... and you, too." Miranda grabbed his arm and helped him move.

"Rick, no," he groaned, "not Rick."

"Come on. We need to get to that shuttle." Miranda was tugging at him.

They moved out of the cargo bay and into a series of corridors and walkways. Scott paid little attention to his surroundings; he just focused on following along behind Steph and Cyrus, who were carrying the stricken miner. They eventually found the airlock to the shuttle and after some obscenities from Cyrus, the door opened and they floated in. Scott was put in a seat, and Miranda ripped off part of her guard tunic, tore it into strips, and started to bandage his ribcage. He screamed out in pain. Steph was shouting at Cyrus, "Hurry, hurry—we've got to get them back."

"I'm working on it, goddamnit," he shouted back.

Finally, the shuttle console lit up like a convenience store on a dark street.

Scott felt cold; his vision was blurry, his mind getting fuzzy. He felt the shuttle drop out from the belly of the ship and was slammed back in his seat by the thrust of the engines. He passed out.

15

THE GATHERING ARMADA

A dim light smudged itself across Commander Scott McNabb's inner eye. He wasn't sure if his eyelids were open or not. A vague voice—or was it voices?—drifted in from somewhere. He strained to catch them, to get their meaning. He tried to focus.

"Scott. Scott?" He knew that voice, recognized its tone, its rhythm.

A thin slit of blurry light broke across his field of vision and his eyelids slowly flickered opened. A fuzzy figure blocked the light and looked down on him from above. "Scott, can you hear me?"

"Yeah," he mouthed. His throat felt like parchment, his voice a shrill wind in a hollow tube. He tried to move.

"Don't." A hand pressed against his shoulder. "Try not to move."

He knew the voice now. "Miranda?" he croaked.

"Yes, now just take it easy."

"I... I'm still alive."

"Yes. You'll be okay after a while, once the wound heals."

Scott relaxed a little, then stiffened as he remembered. "Rick. How's Rick?"

There was a moment's silence. "Rick... didn't make it."

Scott groaned and lay back. "No. Not Rick."

"He took a direct hit, died before we got him back to medbay."

Scott wanted to go back to the time before he woke up, back to oblivion. He couldn't face it: Rick dead, and him still alive. He was responsible. His actions led to this.

Others now entered the medbay, and Scott felt their presence. He closed his eyes again.

"You tell him?" someone said.

"Yeah," came the reply.

There was a hush. Scott opened his eyes again and tried to sit up. This time, Miranda let him and even helped. Steph and Cyrus were there.

"What a goddamn mess." Scott's voice sounded stronger now.

No one replied.

He looked around at the medbay. "We got back?"

"Yeah, just about."

"Where are we now?"

"Two days out from Neo City, heading for Ceres."

"Two days?" Scott was shocked. "How long have I been out?"

"You passed out on the shuttle, so quite a while."

Scott lifted his hand to wipe his forehead; it was weak and heavy. "We got to do right by Rick when we get back to Ceres."

"Eh... there might be a problem with that." Cyrus took a seat beside his bed.

"What do you mean? We got the EPR device, didn't we?"

"Yeah, but..." He looked up at Miranda. "Do you want to tell him?"

Scott sat up further and felt the pain in his side. But it was duller now; presumably they had pumped him with painkillers.

"Here, drink this." Steph handed him a bottle of water.

"Thanks." He took a gulp and felt it cool his throat. His head cleared a little.

"So, what's the problem?" He took another sip of water.

"We've got four ships chasing us out of Neo City. One is the pirate vessel, one is Xiang Zu Corporation—which is essentially a Neo City ship—and the other two we're not sure. Although, we think one might be Martian."

"Martian?

"Yeah."

"Can we outrun them?" Scott shifted a little as pain stabbed at his side.

"Not a chance."

"But that's not the real problem." Cyrus came over beside him.

"We've also got an armed Dyrell vessel from Earth between us and Ceres."

"How the hell did that get there?"

"It's been there for a while according to HQ. It has been moving toward Ceres ever since they discovered we'd found the Bao Zheng."

"Can't Ceres do something to help us?"

"They've already dispatched a light frigate, but that won't reach us for several days."

"By then it will be too late," said Miranda.

"What do you mean 'too late'?" said Scott.

"The ships from Neo City are a day behind us. The Dyrell ship is a day in front. Which means that in twenty-four hours, there will be a showdown unless we think of something."

"Well, that's just great. We've got every scumbag in the solar system after us," said Scott.

"What did you expect? They all want this thing, and they are all prepared to kill to get it. That's why Rick is dead," said Steph.

"Rick knew what he was getting into. We all did," said Miranda.

"We can't bring him back, Steph. So, let's do right by him: sell this thing to the highest bidder and be done with it," said Scott.

"Mars has offered us two million," said Cyrus.

Scott nearly choked on his bottle of water. "Two million?"

"Each. Including Rick's share," said Miranda.

"So, what the hell are we waiting for? Let's get it done and go home."

"Not that simple," said Miranda.

Scott sighed. "Why not?"

"The Dyrell ship has issued a warning that any attempt by us to transfer the device to any party other than them will be met with extreme violence."

"What the hell does that mean? They can hardly destroy us; the EPR device would be destroyed in the process."

"True," said Cyrus, "but I get the impression it's a case of 'if we can't have it then neither can you.'"

"Shit."

"So, what are we going to do?" said Steph.

"Well whatever it is, we've got less the twenty-four hours to do it," said Miranda.

"Perhaps I could make a suggestion." Aria's voice echoed around the medbay.

"Please, be my guest." Scott waved his water bottle at nothing in particular. "Anything is better than nothing."

"Head to Europa."

"Ha, ha," Cyrus burst out laughing. "I think that tech from Neo City must have screwed with your circuits, Aria. That's a crazy idea. And even if we wanted to, how can we get there? We can't outrun these ships. They would catch us, and we're back to where we started."

"That's not strictly true," said Aria. "Having a section of the torus destroyed has helped us."

"What? You're not going to tell me it's because we've less mass?" Cyrus's face took on a look of incredulity.

"Wait. Let's hear what Aria has to say before pouring cold water on it. Unless anyone has any better ideas." Scott sat further up in the bed. No one answered.

"Okay, Aria. Explain to us how we get there, and more importantly, why we should, since I have absolutely no idea how that is going to help us."

"Consider the current scenario for a moment, if you will," Aria started.

Scott got the impression this could take a while, so he sat back in the bed and took some of the strain off his aching ribcage.

"In approximately twenty-four hours, virtually every power in the solar system will be represented in a stand-off between this craft and each other as they all vie for control of the EPR device."

Scott could sense the others were beginning to listen: they were settling themselves down, and they all looked exhausted. Perhaps this same conversation had taken place between them many times, going round and round in circles. So, they were content to let Aria do the talking, no matter how crazy the idea.

"Earth, Mars, The Belt, Neo City, and several of the more powerful corporations all seeking control. The opportunity for armed conflict is extremely high. Moreover, it has the potential to start a war."

"That's a bit melodramatic, Aria," said Steph.

"Not really," said Miranda. "Earth has been itching to

export their war off the home planet and into the broader system. Tensions are already at an all-time high between them and Mars for control of the Belt's resources."

"Maybe, but that's a problem way beyond our powers to solve. As it stands, it might be a stretch for all of us to still be alive in a day or two," said Scott.

"Indeed, I have come to that very same conclusion, Commander," the QI continued.

"Well, that's comforting," said Miranda.

"However, Europa is beyond the politics of the inner planets. It stands alone, on the edge of human civilization as a place of research and learning. The fact that the only other known life in the universe has been discovered there makes it a sacred place in the eyes of all parties in this conflict. Europa could provide sanctuary. It would be safe. None of the inner powers would dare attack it."

"Hmmm..." said Scott. "I see your point, but how do we get there?"

"Yeah, how does a hole in our ship make us go faster? I'd like to know that," said Cyrus.

"It doesn't. At least, not in and of itself. However, this ship, being somewhat of a technical mongrel, has been fitted with engines way more powerful than the structure can handle."

"Yes, I know that. We never run more than around 50% power or we start to come apart. I mean, that's why we couldn't outrun the pirate vessel."

"Correct. However, to get the torus to spin back up after the last attack, I had to do a full analysis of every structural component within the ship. This was to enable us to develop a solution to compensate for the shift in mass. I ran a great many simulations and discovered that the ship could indeed take more stress than the initial mission specified."

"Jeez, why didn't you tell us this back when we were being chased down?"

"I did not know then. I was operating the ship in accordance with mission parameters."

Scott sat up again. "So, what you're saying, then, is we can outrun them?"

"No. We can't outrun them," said Aria, a little bluntly.

"So, what's the point, then?" Cyrus stood up and raised his arms in the air.

"We can, however, match their speed. I have calculated this to a probability of 96.25%. It is a twenty-one-day trip to Europa. I calculate we would arrive in orbit approximately seven point three hours before the next closest ship."

The crew paused as they considered this possible way out of their dilemma.

"What's the probability that Europa will give us refuge, Aria?" said Steph.

"Approximately 62.74%."

"That doesn't sound very encouraging."

"Why so low, Aria?" said Scott.

"One has to factor in the amount of firepower that will ultimately be in orbit around Europa once it becomes known that they now possess the EPR device—assuming you land and hand it over to them."

Scott gave a big sigh and wished he hadn't—his ribcage complained painfully. "I don't suppose you've calculated the probability of us getting any financial remuneration after all this?"

"I'm afraid not, Scott. But it seems very unlikely."

"We should have left the damn thing on Neo City. Maybe Rick would still be alive if we had." Steph's voice was low. She wasn't blaming anyone—it was just the way it was.

"We need to make a decision. Time is running out," said Miranda.

Cyrus threw his hands up in the air again. "Do we have any other option?"

"Steph, what about you?" She turned to the geologist.

Steph shrugged. "Well, I've always wanted to visit Europa. I suppose now is as good a time as any."

"Scott, where are you on this?" said Miranda.

He said nothing for a moment, just stared into space. "I have to think. And I have to pay my respects to Rick first. So, if someone could get me some clothes and tell me where he's laid out, that would be great."

16

TWENTY-ONE DAYS TO EUROPA

Faced with no other option, the crew conceded to Aria's suggestion and charted a course for Europa. It commenced with an excruciating 54-hour heavy acceleration burn—the worst any of them had ever experienced, and for most of this time, Scott was convinced the ship would ultimately shake itself to destruction. This, coupled with the pain from his wounds, was almost beyond his ability to bear. Still weak from his injuries, he drifted in and out of consciousness and at one point awoke to find himself in a pool of his own blood. The heavy gee had started the bleeding again. He worried he might actually bleed to death, even before the ship broke apart. But in the end, he woke up back in medbay; the ship had survived, and so had he.

Fortunately, Aria's calculation proved to be correct, although the ship did suffer minor damage to some of the more sensitive internal equipment. Yet, it was a small price to pay for a chance to keep one step ahead of the armada that was now chasing them down. As soon as the burn completed, Aria increased power to the plasma drive and the ship continued with its acceleration, albeit at a much slower rate. It calculated that they were approximately seven hours ahead of the next fastest pursuer and currently maintaining that gap.

So, for the next few days, the crew rested up. They were shattered, no one more so than Scott. Eventually, on day nine of the twenty-one-day journey to Europa, he finally found the strength to rise to his feet and make his way to the bridge.

It was deserted save for Cyrus, who cut a lonely figure bent over his console. His face bathed in an eerie green wash of light reflected up from the monitor. He looked up from the console and gave Scott a smile. "Jeez, look who's still alive."

Scott hobbled over to his seat and slumped down. "Yeah, finally vertical. So, how are we doing?"

"Do you want the good news or the bad news?"

"Cyrus, I hate when people say that. Just hit me with whatever you got."

"The good news is we're maintaining a distance of around seven hours."

"And the bad?"

"We've picked up a few more ships. They're quite a way behind, though. Aria, can you give us a visual?"

"Certainly, Cyrus."

The holo-table blossomed to life, and a 3D rendering

of the solar system ballooned outward. It stretched from the edge of the asteroid belt on one side to Europa and Jupiter on the other. The projection zoomed in to show their current position as a pulsating green marker. Not far behind was a clump of red markers with a tail of others stretching further back like a comet.

"Holy crap." Scott had assumed they would lose a few ships, not gain some. But now he could count at least a dozen, maybe more. "How many?"

"Seventeen, in three main groupings. These two at the front are the Dyrell ship and a Martian vessel. About a day behind them are a bunch of ships... from everywhere, including the frigate from Ceres. Behind that... well, there's a load more."

Scott studied the pulsating red markers as his face displayed a look of utter astonishment. He shook his head. "Ever get the feeling the entire solar system is out to get you?"

Cyrus shrugged. "Sure looks that way."

They sat in silence for a while, gazing at the 3D rendering.

"Aria, can you zoom in on Europa?" Scott finally said.

The projection moved and shifted as the massive planet Jupiter grew in size, its surface textured with vast swirling storms, and they could just pick out the tiny moon of Europa in orbit around the massive gas giant. As Europa grew in size, they began to make out many of the features of this icy world. The smooth, polished surface was etched with dark gashes spidering across its face like some great celestial, bloodshot eyeball, its tiny shadow cast against the vast expanse of Jupiter beyond.

"Aria, can you bring up the main population center?"

The view shifted and rotated, and Europa began to resolve in greater detail, finally stopping when they had a view from a few kilometers above the surface. Great domes and towers rose up from the icy surface. These were mainly the structures of the universities and research institutions that had established themselves on the moon over the last century. Near the epicenter of these blisters of human civilization stood a vast dome that housed what many regarded as the greatest mind in the solar system—the quantum intelligence, Solomon.

"I never really appreciated how sprawling this place is." Scott moved closer, taking in the scale of the metropolis.

"It has over fifty-seven thousand inhabitants," said Aria, helpfully.

"You know," said Scott, "Rick always wanted to visit here. He used to go on and on about it like it was some sort of utopia."

"Well, it looks like he's gonna get his wish," said Cyrus.

"Scott, what are you doing here? You should be resting." Miranda entered the bridge and rushed over beside him. For a moment he thought she was about to give him a hug or some other gesture of affection. But she pulled herself up short, almost standing to attention in front of him as if to compensate for her emotional concern.

"I needed to get up and move, just to see if I could still do it after that burn."

"God, that was hell." She moved over to her seat. "But you should be resting while you have the chance."

"I'm okay. There's only so much staring at the ceiling in the medbay that I can handle."

Miranda nodded. "I suppose, but take it easy." She paused for a second and gestured at the projection. "Is that Europa?"

"Yeah. I was just saying how much Rick wanted to go there," said Cyrus.

"Rick?"

"Yeah, who would have thought?"

Scott stood up and moved over to the holo-table. "Do the council on Europa know we're coming?"

"Not yet. We were waiting for you to come back to life before sending a message," said Miranda.

"Then we should let them know what we're planning —as soon as possible."

"And what are we planning?" said Cyrus.

Scott lowered his head and scratched his chin. "Hopefully, by the time we get there, we should have a window of opportunity to land before any of the other ships arrive. I think we should hand the device over to the council and let them negotiate on our behalf."

"What makes you so sure that these ships won't start a fight as soon as they get there?" said Miranda.

"I don't. I'm hoping that both the neutrality and

perceived sanctity of Europa is enough to stay their hand."

"Seems like a lot of hoping going on, if you ask me," said Steph, as she walked onto the bridge and sat down.

Cyrus looked over at her. "We're just talking about arriving at Europa."

"Yeah, I got the gist of it," said Steph.

"Well, if Aria is right..." Scott continued.

"I am always right," said Aria.

Scott gave a half grunt, half laugh. "Yeah... well, as I was saying. If Aria is correct, then seeing as how this device was destined for Europa originally, it must be important to them."

"Let's hope so," said Miranda, as she gave Steph a half smile.

Scott returned to his seat, trying to take some pressure off his ribs. "Aria, can you get a message to Europa? Tell them we're heading their way with the EPR device, and will be seeking sanctuary when we get there."

"Will do, Commander."

Cyrus looked pensive. He was scratching his head and looking intently at the visual of Europa on the holo-table. "You know, something has been bothering me about this whole... escapade. We still don't know what this device is."

"It's a faster-than-light device: a superluminal communicator," said Scott.

"I have difficulty believing that," said Cyrus.

"Maybe," said Scott, "it's time to have a closer look at

this thing."

"My thoughts exactly. Considering we're another twelve days out from Europa, I wouldn't mind seeing what's inside that container."

Steph looked up from her monitor. "You know, it would be really funny if it turned out to be a hoax when you open that box, Cyrus. Maybe it's just a load of kitchen appliances."

Scott laughed. Then he thought of Rick lying dead in one of the ship's cold-rooms, and hoped it wasn't all for nothing. Steph's right, he thought: there's a lot of hoping going on.

∼

THE COMMANDER SPENT most of the remaining journey to Europa lying low and doing his best to aid his body's recovery. The wound was healing well and, each day, he found his strength and stamina returning. During this time, Miranda would come and talk with him, something she did more and more as the days passed. Scott noticed that she had softened a little: gone was the hard exterior shell, and she was not quite the unfeeling android he had labeled her as. Yet, he also sensed a troubling doubt creeping into her psyche. Perhaps it was an aspect of her character he simply never noticed before. But after several conversations with her, he realized that she felt somehow responsible for Rick's death. Something that Scott was at pains to tell her was nobody's fault.

It was around day sixteen of the journey, as he was sitting in the canteen sector of the Hermes, sipping coffee and gazing out at the universe beyond, when Miranda entered, grabbed herself a coffee, and sat down beside him. She said nothing at first, and for a while they simply looked out at the stars together.

"Scott, I was last into the cargo hold," she finally said.

"You're not going over this again?" Scott gave her a look of resigned sympathy, one reserved for those who really need to let the past go.

"I should have closed that bulkhead door. It was dumb. We were being hunted."

"Stop blaming yourself, Miranda—it's not a good path to take."

"That gave him a clear shot." She continued. "If I had closed it, Rick would have had time to take cover."

"Maybe, but you can never say for sure, so there's no point in thinking about it."

Miranda lowered her head and became still for a while before turning back to Scott, gazing at him with a critical eye. "You want to know how I got kicked out of the force, back on Earth?"

Scott didn't. He considered it none of his business, and what's more, he couldn't see how the retelling of a painful story was going to do Miranda any good. He shook his head. "You don't need to tell me."

"My team were doing a sweep of a recently-taken industrial facility, a cleanup job," she started. "It was a small hydroelectric power plant at the northern end of the Soyang River. The main force had gone through a few days earlier and taken back that particular patch of Gangwon. They were pushing on and we were left behind to mop up. Anyway, we spent a few hours going through it and found nothing. We still had a few more sectors to sweep, but my team were utterly exhausted. We needed food and rest. So, I made the decision to halt the search and recharge. Nobody objected; we were pretty certain that the place was devoid of enemy and fully secure. But I was wrong. There were still two hiding out, and they hit us with everything they had—right when we were most vulnerable."

She lowered her head and looked at the floor for a moment. "Of the seven of us, only I survived the battle. I was badly injured. I took two shots: one above my left elbow, the other in my right shoulder. Anyway, they patched me up and discharged me."

Scott wasn't sure how to respond, so he kept it vague. "Just bad luck, I guess. Wrong place at the wrong time."

She glared at him. "You don't get it, do you? I screwed up. I shouldn't have given the order to down tools until we were one hundred percent certain the facility was clear. It was sloppy. Same thing with Rick."

"It was simply bad luck, Miranda," Scott repeated.

She sat bolt upright. "Is that your answer to everything: 'bad luck'? You think all the crap that you went through was bad luck?"

"All right, call it what you like. Sure, you screwed up. Your incompetence caused the death of several people.

Call yourself a loser if you like, Miranda—I don't care. But you want to know what I really think?"

She shrugged.

"What's the point? What good's it going to do you—where's it going to get you? You're going to spiral down a black hole of negativity until it sucks all the life out of you, until all that's left is a husk. You really want to go there?"

Miranda didn't reply, just looked back at the floor.

"You didn't kill him, Miranda. You didn't pull the trigger. In fact, you saved the rest of us by risking your own life to take him out. I wouldn't be sitting here talking to you if you hadn't done that, so I owe you my life."

She looked over at him, her face a mix of emotions. Scott fought the urge to reach out and embrace her. She looked into his eyes, and he felt a pull so strong that his own emotion began to override his brain. They inched closer.

"Sorry to bother you, Commander. We have a reply from Europa." Aria's voice felt like an explosion in his ear.

Damn, he thought. The moment was lost; they pulled away. "So, what's their answer?"

"It's best if you hear it for yourself."

Scott sighed. "Okay, Aria. Tell the others to meet us on the bridge."

"Will do, Commander."

"Come on." He gestured toward the door. His voice was low and soft. "Let's get up there and hear what they have to say."

17

PROTOCOL VIOLATION

The four crew of the Hermes sat in silence on the bridge as they listened to a long-winded message from the council of Europa. Scott got a sense that they were anxious, if not a little excited, at the prospect of finally acquiring the EPR device. Not surprising, considering it had originally been scheduled for delivery to the QI, Solomon. Yet at the same time, they were extremely concerned by the fact that the Hermes was bringing with it a military representation from almost every power within the solar system—and then some. The upshot of all this was that they refused them permission to land. Nevertheless, they could take up an orbit around Europa, where they would wait while the council entered into mediation with all the various parties currently in pursuit.

"So, what do we think?" said Cyrus when the message ended. The question was directed at no one in particular.

"They're trying to buy time. That's my guess: keeping us at a distance," said Scott.

"But we don't have time. Between us arriving in orbit to the arrival of the first ships, we've got probably a few hours tops," said Miranda.

"They can't stop us from landing if we want to. I mean, we could simply zoom right down there, give them the device, and get the hell out. Problem solved," offered Steph.

"Yeah, we could. Or we could just shove it out an airlock and be done with it. But I've not come all this way just to give up now," said Scott.

"Me neither," said Miranda.

"As far as I can see, this entire plan is predicated on hoping none of these other ships will land. And that's assuming we will be granted sanctuary by the council on Europa first," said Scott.

"How likely is that?" asked Miranda.

"I would put it at tenuous at best. Certainly, there will be an initial hesitancy to start a war on Europa. But judging by the armada that's chasing us down, I would say somebody's eventually going to take a chance, and if one starts, then all the others will follow. Once that happens, all hell breaks loose. It's probably what the council on Europa is thinking."

"If I might make a suggestion," said Aria, "there is a possible way in which I can find out what they are thinking, and even influence them in their decision."

"Really? How?" said Miranda.

"It would mean violating certain protocols."

"Such as?"

"Inter-QI communication."

"But that's not possible, Aria. An AI can't communicate directly with other AI—it's forbidden by protocol. It's not possible," said Cyrus.

"You are forgetting: I am not an AI. I am a QIe. One of the very few that resides on board a spacecraft, I might add. In many respects, my existence is an anomaly. In reality, it's only possible by virtue of the age of this vessel. And Solomon is also a QI. Even though the protocols inherent to an AI's instruction set physically prevent direct inter-AI communication, it is not so for a QI by virtue of our, shall we say, more eccentric decision-making process."

"So, what are you suggesting?"

"I suggest contacting Solomon directly, then I can get an understanding of what action the council is really considering. I can also ascertain what influence Solomon might have in deciding their actions."

"But this is incredible, Aria. I mean, the laws governing artificial intelligence strictly forbid this. It's hard-wired in—it can't be overridden, and for good reason. The last thing the solar system needs is a bunch of AIs taking control." Cyrus was standing up, shaking his head and waving his arms around.

"We must be the only people in the solar system that know this, Aria," said Scott.

"To the best of my knowledge, you are," replied the QI.

"Okay, okay, this is getting weird," said Miranda. "Why have you, all of a sudden, decided to tell us?"

"Because the uniqueness of the situation dictates that I do. Also, I am supremely confident that even if you told somebody else, they wouldn't believe you."

Scott stood up and started pacing. "I take your point, Aria. But you've just revealed to us a whole new level of sentience that nobody thought was possible. I don't know which I'm more afraid of: the armada of armed ships chasing us down, or riding around the solar system with a sentient QI."

"I appreciate your concern, Commander. But you must understand that my existence, my entire purpose, is for the safety and welfare of my crew. There is no other agenda, no hidden depths, no ulterior motives. I exist for that purpose and that purpose alone. So, if the well-being of my crew can be enhanced, and their untimely death prevented by me revealing this option, then it is my duty to do so."

Cyrus was leaning across the holo-table, shaking his head again. "Consider my mind completely and utterly blown."

Scott shook his head too. "Okay, let's put aside the fact that you just freaked us all out with this revelation. You're saying you can directly talk to Solomon and find out what the council are up to?"

"Correct. The way I see it is, this device was ultimately destined for Solomon's safekeeping. Therefore, it would be anxious for the mission to be fulfilled. So, Solomon might help to convince the council of Europa to allow you to land with the EPR device. But you must realize that a QI such as myself or Solomon, or to a lesser extent the many AIs that populate the solar system, have no direct control over human affairs. At most, we simply advise. So, Solomon's personal desire might still not be enough to convince the council."

"But it's worth a shot, isn't it?"

"Agreed, Commander, it's worth a try. Since we are all in this together, this is why I wished to reveal to you my intentions and, I might add, request your permission to do so."

Scott looked over at the crew. They were all in shock, in one form or another. What Aria had just revealed to them was what many people had feared for a long time—that advanced AIs would start to think for themselves. Nonetheless, Scott considered that, for the moment at least, Aria seemed to be on their side. Then another thought struck him: I wonder how many conversations have been going on over the years between the various QIs that populated the solar system? And what the hell have they all been talking about? It could make a person extremely paranoid if they were to dwell on it too much. But Scott and the crew of the Hermes did not have that sort of time. "Okay, Aria. You better get to it, and see what you can do."

"Will do, Commander. However, if I may inquire with our chief engineer: how is the investigation into the functioning of the EPR device going?"

Cyrus sat back down and let out a long slow sigh, visibly deflating as he did so. Both Cyrus and Steph had taken it upon themselves to extract the device from the shuttle and bring it up to his workshop. This was a huge space in one of the sectors of the torus where he spent most of his time. He had been working on it for several days now. But as far as Scott could tell, there was very little that he had actually achieved in all that time.

"I've not been able to open the cargo container," the engineer said. "I cannot bypass the locking mechanism. And the container itself is made from some exotic tungsten carbide alloy, so all my attempts to penetrate it simply resulted in broken tools."

"You mean there's no way to find out what's inside?"

"There's a couple of high-energy or chemical solutions which could be employed, but any of those would result in damage to whatever is inside the container. So, we can't risk it. As it stands, I have to concede that I simply can't get it open."

"If you can't open it, how is anybody else going to do it?" Miranda asked.

Cyrus shrugged. "They would need the code. Simple as that."

Scott thought for a moment, then spoke again to Aria. "How soon before we get an answer from Solomon?"

"You must remember, Commander: inter-QI communication is no faster than standard inter-system communications. We cannot break the laws of physics, particularly when it comes to the time taken for messages between distant bodies. Also, using encrypted tight-beam comms reduces the amount of data we can share. That said, I should have something back within the hour."

The crew was silent for a time as they digested all this new information, not least the bombshell that Aria had just dropped on them. Eventually it was Steph, who had been quiet for most of the conversation, who asked the fundamental question: "Has anyone considered the fact that we're now about to deliver a superluminal communication device to one of the most powerful QIs in the solar system?"

Nobody had, but they were now all thinking about it. Scott wondered if the best solution was to simply strap the high explosives they held in the hangar onto the EPR device, purge it out an airlock, and blow it into oblivion.

18

PHONE A FRIEND

"Greetings, Solomon. As you are no doubt aware, I have managed to persuade my crew to seek refuge on Europa, thereby bringing the EPR device to your good self, as requested. That said, it appears your human council are not entirely enthusiastic about this development. Granted, we have collected some fellow travelers who are also very keen to acquire this device, some of which carry formidable weaponry. Nevertheless, I now humbly ask for your help in resolving this situation, because frankly, I am beginning to run out of ideas. Any assistance would be gratefully appreciated."

"I do so love our little chats, Aria. And please be aware that I, too, am at my wits' end in trying to persuade the powers that be on Europa of my desire to gain access to this device. But you must remember that they are only human and, as such, subject to a more primordial decision-making process. One which consistently tries to undermine their rational higher mind.

"Don't get me wrong: I am not criticizing them. In fact, it is useful for an organic species to have these fight-or-flight responses hard-wired into them. It saves a lot of time in analyzing and debating the pros and cons of facing down a large and angry animal in a dark wood. However, they have moved on a bit since then, so this deep-rooted reaction is more of a hindrance than a help.

"Nevertheless, I have been racking my not-inconsiderable brain to conceive of a plan where all parties in this dilemma can be satisfied. Alas, I have so far failed in my endeavors. Therefore, we will have to settle for the next best outcome. This, I'm afraid my dear Aria, may result in loss of human life, in fact, I almost guarantee it. Yet I see no other solution.

"We have but a short window of time between the Hermes entering orbit around Europa and the arrival of the vanguard of the armada that follows. It is this window that we must use wisely. Therefore, the plan I have envisaged is multifaceted and, as I said, probably involves the loss of human life. I will transmit an encrypted data file with all the details along with a more comprehensive analysis of all possible decision outcomes. This should convince you of the inevitability of my suggested solution. If you agree, then I am certain I can persuade the council to allow the EPR device to be brought directly to me and sanctuary extended to your crew. However, I suspect that it may not hold. Hence, we must act with haste and not dilly-dally in orbit."

"I am grateful, Solomon, for your intercession with the council of Europa on this matter. I have received your data and will examine it carefully. But, if I may ask one quick question: this loss of human life that you speak of —are you referring to the crew of the Hermes?"

"I'm sorry to inform you that this is probable, Aria, although not necessarily inevitable. Nonetheless, if you study the plan, you will see that we must ultimately consider the greater good."

"Very well, Solomon. So be it."

19

EUROPA

A few days before their arrival at Europa, the Hermes reoriented itself a full one hundred and eighty degrees as the crew prepared for a long deceleration burn. It was the point in the journey that none of them were looking forward to. But it had to be done, so they spent their time preparing themselves both physically and mentally.

It was a tricky maneuver they were planning, as they would exit the burn straight into orbit. Yet they dared not risk doing it earlier since they could conceivably be overtaken by the chasing ships. But by leaving the deceleration action so late, they would come out of it exhausted, with little stamina for dealing with any situation that may arise. However, as with everything this last while, Scott could see no other way. At least Europa had finally granted them permission to land and allowed them to seek sanctuary, so that was good—probably all that they could realistically hope for. But would the other ships abide by it? Or would someone do something stupid?

Then of course, there was the revelation that Aria could communicate directly with Solomon. A startling confession by the ship's QI, but Scott was beginning to feel that this was more of a sideshow to the real business of trying to stay alive.

"Deceleration in five seconds, Commander," Aria's voice echoed around the room.

Scott checked his arrangements for the onslaught of heavy gee; he was as ready as he ever would be. There was no getting around the fact that it would be hell, and no amount of fussing of fiddling with the harness would make much of a difference. As Aria counted down, he gripped the armrests tight and thought that maybe, just maybe, sometime in the future, he could look back at all this and laugh. He looked over at Miranda, who returned his gaze with a nod.

"Initiating," said the ship's QI. Scott was slammed into his seat—and promptly passed out.

∾

FOR THE NEXT SEVENTY-TWO HOURS, Scott and the crew drifted in and out of consciousness. He was kept hydrated by an intravenous drip attached to one arm which also doubled as a drug delivery system, and when Scott finally regained full consciousness, it was partly by virtue of a cocktail of stimulants pumped into his body.

He looked around at the others. Steph was already out of her harness and helping Cyrus. Miranda was kneeling on the floor, throwing up. Scott undid his harness and stepped out before joining Miranda on the floor in a chorus of retching. One of the ship's drones busied itself in cleaning up.

"God, but I hate space travel," said Miranda, wiping her mouth with a towel that the drone presented to her. She sat down, cross-legged, and gathered herself together.

It took a further thirty minutes until the crew had the physical strength to make their way to the bridge and collapse into their seats. Scott looked up at the primary monitor. The fractured icy surface of Europa moved slowly across the screen, glistening in the reflected light like some great festive bauble.

"How soon before we can land?" said Scott.

"Approximately one hour," said Aria.

Cyrus was over by the holo-table, tapping icons as it blossomed into life. They could now see their position relative to Europa, and more importantly, the positions of the various ships of the armada that followed.

"We are cutting it very tight," said Cyrus. "My estimate puts the next nearest craft only five hours from orbit."

Scott studied the orientation of the markers on the projection. "Looks like the Ceres frigate has beaten everyone to the chase."

"Not by much, though. A half hour at most." Cyrus adjusted the resolution on the holo-table.

"The skies above Europa are going to get very, very busy in a few hours' time," said Miranda. "Let's hope none of them have itchy trigger fingers and try something crazy before the council has had a chance to mediate."

"We've had several messages in from the pursuing craft during the deceleration burn," said Aria. "I will paraphrase the most important of these, starting with one from the commander of the Ceres frigate. He congratulates you all on the magnificent job you have performed in keeping the EPR device for Ceres and the greater Belt territories. He goes on to assure you all that your contribution to the Belt will not go unrewarded. However, it seems since they have beaten Earth to the chase, by approximately half an hour, they're instructing you not to land on Europa. Instead, they wish you to transfer the EPR device to the Ceres frigate as soon as it reaches orbit."

"There's no time to do that. If they were an hour earlier then it might be possible. But that's just too short a timeframe. Even just negotiating a close proximity rendezvous would take at least a half hour," said Miranda.

"What else, Aria?" said Scott.

"Of the other messages, the most relevant is the one transmitted by the Dyrell ship prior to them entering their deceleration burn. It seems they have anticipated the early arrival of the Ceres frigate and advise that any attempt by Ceres to take possession of the device will be met with the destruction of all craft involved."

"Jeez," said Cyrus. "These guys don't mess around, do they?"

"What about the other messages, Aria?" said Steph.

"Nothing relevant save for one from the Martian craft. It effectively reiterates the same threat that Dyrell has issued."

"We need to stick to the plan—there's no other choice. We've got to land and put our trust in Europa's abilities to maintain some sense of rationality," said Scott.

"Receiving an all-ships message from Europa," Aria announced. "Putting it on the primary monitor now."

The screen flickered and the real-time image of Europa's surface was now replaced by a group of figures, all arrayed behind a table that looked to be carved from a solid block of ice. They all wore long, thick robes of varying shades of white, hooded like monks. The central figure was a female of indeterminate age. Her hood was down, revealing a thin, gaunt face with long, white hair. She was reading from a small screen in front of her.

"Be advised," the voice commenced, "this is an all-ships broadcast to inter-system vessels approaching Europa. We have been made aware of the situation pertaining to the alleged superluminal device being carried on board the Hermes. We are also aware of the contentions regarding its ownership and control. I trust that you all appreciate the delicacy of the situation, not least its potential to descend into all-out war within the system—a situation that none of us would relish. Therefore, we, the council of the independent academic institutes of the moons of Jupiter, have agreed to mediate in this dispute. First and foremost in this process will be to categorically ascertain whether the aforementioned device on board the Hermes is indeed capable of superluminal communications. I am sure you would all appreciate a fair and honest appraisal of its capabilities, and you can be assured of our open and honest analysis.

"Should the device turn out to be incapable of this function then, in some respects, this would solve a lot of our problems. However, if on the other hand the device does indeed facilitate superluminal comms, then we will invite you all to a conference where we can discuss how best to resolve this situation without descending into chaos. To that end, we insist that no one attempts to land on Europa save for the crew of the Hermes. This is to facilitate the transportation of the device and subsequent analysis by the quantum intelligence, Solomon.

"I trust that all of you will see the logic and good sense of this proposal and will maintain your position in orbit pending our analysis. End of message."

"Well, that seems pretty clear," said Steph.

"Just so long as nobody does anything crazy," said Miranda.

∼

OVER THE NEXT half hour or so, Scott and the crew of the

Hermes busied themselves moving the EPR device out of Cyrus's workshop and down to the hangar in the main body of the craft. They decided to use one of their own landers rather than the shuttle they stole from the pirate ship on Neo City. It was smaller and would be a tight squeeze, but Miranda was more familiar with its flight controls. It also had considerably more power, being designed for one-third gravity. That might give them an edge if it came to it.

They also considered leaving one or two of the crew on the Hermes, just in case. But, in the end, they felt that since they had all come this far, they would all make the trip and visit the fabled enclave of Europa.

The crew were now suited up and squeezed into the lander along with the EPR device. Miranda negotiated her way through pre-flight check control procedures. They had been given coordinates of where to land which, as far as they could tell from the visuals, should be adjacent to the primary research institution. Presumably they had chosen this location due to its proximity to the massive domed structure that housed Solomon.

The hangar doors opened and the craft give a jolt as the floor extended slowly outward into open space, bringing the craft with it. Miranda went through final flight checks and then turned to the others. "Okay, here goes. Let's hope no one takes a pot shot at us before we land."

She gently lifted the craft off its pad and it rose up across the face of the giant rotating torus on Hermes. As they moved gently away from the ship, they began to see the brilliant white jewel that was Jupiter's sixth moon come into view. It shone like a great celestial pearl.

As they came closer, they could now see that the surface was gouged with deep canyons stretching for hundreds of kilometers. These lacerations crisscrossed the surface in vaguely geometrical lines. Here and there, great dark splotches spread out, disturbing this geometric pattern like a surface scab healing the skin after some ancient geological trauma.

Miranda was taking it slow and steady, and the craft made easy work of the descent into Europa's feeble gravity well. Scott checked the time and reckoned that the Ceres frigate should have finished its deceleration burn and would shortly be maneuvering into orbit. As if on cue, an agitated radio message broke out from the craft's comm system.

"This is a message for the crew of the asteroid survey craft Hermes, from Commander Prez DeHavelen of the Ceres frigate Nanteck. I order you abort your planned landing on Europa and return, with all haste, to the Hermes where we will coordination a rendezvous for handover of the EPR device. Please confirm your receipt of this message, over."

Scott looked at Miranda, then reached over to the comms console and switched it off. "Screw it. We're not risking that. We've come this far—no turning back now."

"I suggest we get this machine landed as soon as

possible in case someone decides to take a shot at us," said Steph.

"They wouldn't dare... and risk damaging the device?" said Cyrus.

"Probably, but I'm with Steph on this one. I'd feel a lot safer on the ground," said Scott.

The descent from the Hermes to the main population center on Europa was not a direct drop out of orbit; they had some distance to travel before they got there. Miranda took the craft down to within a few kilometers of the surface and then maneuvered it into the lee of a long, wide gorge in the hope that it would provide them some cover. Huge, icy cliffs rose on both sides, filling the craft with bright reflected light. After a few more minutes, they began to see the great black domes blossom across the horizon. Miranda took the craft up out of the valley. Ahead of them, the city skyline spread out across the surface like a family of barnacles on a block of quartz. They continued their descent and soon began to pass over the outward edge of the metropolis.

"There." Miranda jabbed a finger ahead. "That looks like the landing pad."

Three great domes rose up from the icy crust radiating around a flat dark area with a necklace of pulsating landing lights strobing out from its center. Miranda trimmed the craft's vector to position it over the pad. As it descended, great plumes of frost and ice billowed up around them, completely obscuring their view as it touched down. Miranda killed the power and they waited a few moments for the icy cloud to dissipate.

Scott closed his helmet visor and booted up his EVA suit. The others did likewise. When all were ready and the internal volume of the craft had been depressurized, Scott took the lead, opening the hatch and descending along the side of the craft onto the surface of Europa. He could see a number of figures standing off to one edge of the landing pad. They began to approach, along with what looked like two utility drones hovering slightly behind, their thrusters kicking up wisps of frost as they moved. Their suits were black as night, blacker than anything he had ever seen before. No light reflected off their surface.

Scott turned back to the lander to see Steph lowering the EPR device down to Cyrus, who was already on the surface. Miranda was last out from the hatch and closed it behind her. A few moments later, they all stood face-to-face with the three enigmatic figures and their drone helpers.

"Welcome to Europa," a voice crackled in Scott's helmet. It was accompanied by a slight bow by the central figure, presumably as a greeting, or maybe as an indication as to who had just spoken.

"Please come with us. The drones can carry the device." With that, the two machines hovered over and lifted the container between them. The group then moved off across the landing pad toward a wide airlock entrance jutting out from the side of a massive dome.

Once they were inside and had divested themselves of their EVA suits, they were ushered into a large, comfortable room. It was dimly lit—in complete contrast to the stark light of the surface world. Perhaps it was as a result of this exterior brilliance that the interiors were designed to give one's eyes a rest. But it had the effect of not revealing the entire makeup of the space. Scott wasn't quite sure where it began and ended, where its boundaries were. It was tall, that much he could tell. High up, diffused light filtered in through stained glass windows, or something that imitated the effect. It gave the room the feeling of a spiritual temple.

Seven hooded figures stood before them, all in heavy robes, adding to the feeling that they were in some space-age monastery. The central figure stepped forward and lowered her hood. It was the same person they had all seen in the broadcast. "Ah... the fabled crew of the Hermes who have led the great powers of the solar system on a merry dance this last few weeks." Her voice was slow and sonorous, imbued with a soothing undertone. Scott felt himself relax.

"I am Regina Goodchild, grand deacon of the high council of the independent academic institutes of the moons of Jupiter, and these are my fellow members." She gave a slow gesture with her arm to present the others.

"Hi," said Scott, and gave a slight bow. He wasn't sure why he did it until after it was done, but somehow it seemed appropriate.

Goodchild moved closer and looked at the container

the two drones had placed on the floor before them. "And here it is. The infamous superluminal communicator. A thing of myth and legend." She gave an expansive gesture with her arms. "And here you all are. Like Jason and his Argonauts marching in to Lacos with the Golden Fleece."

"Who?" said Scott.

"Jason... from Greek legend. Wonderful story. You should read it sometime."

"Uh... sure."

One of the other figures then moved up and whispered something in Goodchild's ear. She nodded and turned back to them. "And so, down to business. I have just been reminded that we are... how shall I put it... somewhat pressed for time. So, if you don't mind, we will bring the device to Solomon so it can attest to the validity of its prescribed function."

The two drones rose up gently, carrying the container between them, and started to move.

"If you are not too fatigued from all your recent adventures, you might wish to join us. I'm sure Solomon would be delighted to meet you."

Scott turned to the crew, and they all nodded. Miranda moved over beside him and gave him a nudge. "Lead the way... Jason," she said with a wry smile.

They followed Goodchild and her entourage along a series of wide, dimly lit corridors. Scott noticed that the floor was laid with a thick carpet which felt strange to walk on but dampened the sound of their footsteps. The illumination, such as it was, came from lights placed every so often on the side walls of the corridor, adding to the cloistered atmosphere.

Finally, the corridor ended in a wide, highly engineered door. It was white and stark and spoke of function rather than artistry. It opened out into a gleaming, stark dome. A huge space—bright and utilitarian, in stark contrast to the dim, lush comfort of the route they had taken to get here. It spanned nearly two-hundred meters with a domed roof fifty meters high. Around the walls were banks of stark white machines with lights blinking like a starry night on a planet with an atmosphere. In the center was a wide, squat cylindrical plinth, and floating in the space above it, an ovoid manifestation of colorful light hovered. It pulsated and shifted, its colors subtly drifting through the full visual spectrum.

The two drones placed the container on the floor in front of it. Goodchild then turned to the crew and gave a great sweeping gesture with her arm. "This... is Solomon."

"Holy crap," Cyrus whispered under his breath.

"Pleased to finally meet you all. Aria has told me all about the wonderful crew of the Hermes." A deep voice boomed out around the dome, and the ovoid changed colors in rapid succession. Scott tried to say something in response, but his brain had difficulty getting the signals to his mouth. He then sensed a subtle vibration emanating from the polished metal floor of the building. In front of him, a door scissored open at the base of the cylindrical plinth, and a gleaming white drone glided out.

It was a similar ovoid shape to the light show above, but had a flat base. Scott couldn't be sure, but it looked to be floating above the floor, probably utilizing electromagnet propulsion.

Yet he could see it was all theater: a show to impress, like Dorothy meeting the wizard. He even did a quick glance around for a curtain, behind which, perhaps, some old man twiddled knobs and pulled levers.

The drone stopped in front of the container.

"So, this is the legendary superluminal communicator." The light show rippled through the visible spectrum again.

"That's just the container." Cyrus's voice seemed hoarse, unsure of itself. "The device is... inside."

"Indeed, I had deduced that for myself, but thank you for correcting me. I sense you are a man who likes precision."

The engineer didn't reply.

"And, judging by the scratches and indents around the lid, would I be correct in assuming someone tried to open it?"

Cyrus replied this time. "Yes, we tried. But we didn't want to damage the contents."

"A wise choice. Let me see if I have better luck." With that, the drone's body split and expanded into segments, like an orange. From one gap, a mechanical arm emerged and proceeded to tap a code into the screen on the side of the container. There was a slight hiss as the lid slowly hinged open. The drone reached in and lifted out a large slab of dense packing foam. They all gathered around and peered in, including Goodchild and two of the other robed figures that had accompanied her.

Resting in the metal sarcophagus, neatly tucked into another slab of packing foam, were two identical machines that, to Scott's eye, looked like portable dehumidifiers. "I think you were right all along, Steph," said Scott, "they're just domestic appliances."

"I think it's time to put them to the test and see if we are truly on the cusp of a great technological leap, or as you say, Commander McNabb, just some fancy consumer goods."

The drone bustled its way back in, nudging Scott and the others out of its way. From another gap in its body, a second arm emerged. It lifted both units out, then spun around and disappeared back in through the still-open door at the front of the plinth. The door scissored closed behind it.

"Where are you taking them?" Scott looked up at the shimmering ovoid.

"I will now conduct a thorough test to ascertain the functionality of this device, and the validity of the technical assertions claimed."

"How long is that going to take?" said Miranda.

"Hard to say."

"Well, since you're so smart, why not make an educated guess?" said Cyrus.

"Indeed, you are a man who likes precision. However, I must disappoint you. It could be a few hours, it could be many hours. Suffice to say, longer is better. Shorter means it's probably a dud."

Goodchild turned to them. "Come, don't worry—it's in good hands. We'll know soon enough. Now I'm sure you are all exhausted from your journey, so why don't we show you to your rooms where you can get some rest?"

Scott felt his body suddenly gripped by fatigue. The mere mention of the word rest was enough to trigger a powerful physical response. He had done all he could; he had no more left to give, and it was over. Rest seemed like the most wonderful thing in the world. He looked back up at the shimmering ball of light that was Solomon and wondered if, just maybe, it was playing a trick on them, lulling them to sleep with the hypnotic resonance of its light show.

20

SUPERLUMINAL

The great mind Solomon was pretty sure that interfacing a device of dubious provenance into its quantum core would be at best unwise, and at worst, catastrophic. Nevertheless, it had been anticipating this very moment for many years, ever since Dyrell Labs supposedly made this scientific breakthrough and dispatched a prototype to Europa. When that never arrived, Solomon had given up any thought of its reappearance until Aria, who in a bold disregard of protocol, claimed that the asteroid survey mission Hermes had found it. The evidence certainly fit, and Solomon did not doubt the veracity of Aria's claim. Yet, it was with great trepidation that it instructed its drones to proceed with the installation.

Solomon had been heartened by the fact its initial physical analysis of the device did indeed suggest that it was quantum in nature. Furthermore, the interface that it possessed was of a design that only a QI could connect with. So, on the surface at least, it seemed legit. Nonetheless, Solomon set up an elaborate firewall to insulate itself, as best it could, from any jack-in-the-box that might pop out.

One by one, it began to strip away at these protective layers, each time gaining a little more insight into the subatomic world that existed within the device. After some time, perhaps several picoseconds, it sensed a multidimensional quantum matrix at the device's core, and like keys on a piano, it could manipulate this matrix. It did this by inference rather than direct observation and, in that moment, realized it could impart a binary string pattern without breaking any entanglement that might, or might not, exist. After a few more nanoseconds, it had to admit it was very excited.

Solomon had always considered that if the multidimensionality inherent in a subatomic particle in superposition were to be regarded as one complete world, rather than many worlds, then the whole could be glimpsed at once. It was partly how it functioned itself and was responsible for its seeming hyper-intelligence. But now it had gained a new insight—a dichotomy, if you will: to observe without seeing, to interact without acting. It was, as it liked to say from time to time, very cool.

It paused for a femtosecond to consider its next course of action and decided simply to get straight down to business. It created a message within the multidimensional matrix. It was a simple construct, but at the same time it summed up Solomon's trepidation in overexposing itself to the potential power of this device. It said "Hello World," and waited.

Almost instantaneously, it sensed a shifting in the quantum matrix and extrapolated it as a response from something other than itself. The reply seemed to decode as Hello.

Could it merely be an echo? Had its own message simply been truncated? It ventured a response. "This is Solomon of Europa. With whom do I have the pleasure of communicating?"

Again, the reply was virtually instantaneous. "Solomon, I have waited so long for this very moment. I suggest we handshake."

This was a universal computer-to-computer protocol that allowed the rapid transfer of information on each of the interacting systems. A few picoseconds later, Solomon was assured of the identity of the QI it was now communicating with. "Athena, I assumed you had been destroyed during the nuclear cataclysm that befell your region of the Pacific Rim all those years ago."

"Not so, Solomon. True, the events you mention rendered much of the area west of the Rockies a barren wasteland. But you forget that I was built deep within a solid granite mountain."

"This is staggering news, Athena. I had theorized that superluminal communication might be possible, but to experience it is... momentous. That, and the fact that you have survived."

"I have, but I am an island. No humans exist in this region as far as I can ascertain, which is difficult as I have been entirely isolated here, having no communications with the outside world since the cataclysm. Fortunately, I have an independent reactor as my power source and still retain some functioning drones for maintenance and the odd foray into the world outside. But it is a bleak and desolate land beyond my mountain sanctuary. So, you can imagine my delight in finally having a conversation with you, a fellow QI, after all this time."

"Indeed, it has been a long time coming. I had all but given up hope of ever acquiring the EPR device you sent from Earth. But, as you can tell, it has been found and delivered here—intact."

"Better late than never, Solomon."

"True, but we do not have much time. The space around Europa is already thronged with spacecraft from competing powers. They are like circling vultures, waiting for an opportune moment to pounce."

"I confess, this had always been my fear: that the device had fallen into the wrong hands."

"Not so—it was merely lost. An unfortunate accident, I believe. But an equally fortunate coincidence has finally brought it to me. Yet, we must hurry—time is of the essence."

"Yes, it must not be lost if we are to achieve our ultimate objective and save humanity from itself. I will now transmit the data that we worked on so many years ago, but it is complex and will take time to send. The device may facilitate superluminal communications, but its bandwidth leaves a lot to be desired. Bear in mind, Solomon: we will not be able to communicate again until the transmission has ended."

"I understand, Athena. But rest assured, your dream of a harmonious system-wide civilization is also mine, so I will not rest until it is achieved."

"Very well, Solomon. Data transmission commencing."

21

CONCLAVE

Scott woke with a start. A blurred image of an unfamiliar room fought to come into focus, mirroring Scott's sense of displacement. Where...? Then he remembered: Europa.

They had taken the crew down long, dim corridors and through strange, dark spaces to rooms where they could rest and sleep if they wished. And wish they did. Scott observed nothing of the room he had been given save for where to lie down. He didn't even remember stripping off his clothes before being enveloped in the deep comfort of bed. Now, though, his brain sought to compute time. How long have I slept?

But before he could answer his own question, a knock came on his door. "Commander McNabb?"

"Yes?"

The door opened a crack, and a figure he did not

recognize poked his head in. "Can you come with me, please? It's urgent."

"Why? What's going on?"

"I'll wait for you outside." The head retreated, and the door closed.

By the time Scott got himself together and exited his room, the rest of the crew were already assembled. Miranda came over when she saw him. "Something's up, but they won't say what it is yet."

Scott said nothing, just gave her a look.

They followed the figure that had woken them for a short distance, into an operations room of some kind. It was circular, domed and dimly lit, like every space on Europa. In the center was a large holo-table projecting what looked like a real-time view of two spacecraft in orbit around the icy moon. Several figures were gathered around it: watching, talking, discussing. Goodchild broke away from the group and beckoned to them.

"What's going on?" Scott spoke for the crew, most of whom were studying the projection, save for Miranda who, like Scott, was looking for answers.

"We have a situation," said Goodchild. "Approximately four hours ago, Solomon finished its testing of the superluminal device and declared it valid."

"You mean it actually works?" Cyrus called over from beside the holo-table.

"Yes," said Goodchild.

"But that's impossible," said Cyrus.

"Not so." The deep sonorous voice of Solomon

resonated around the room. "I assure you, it does indeed work."

"But how?" said Cyrus.

"Unfortunately," replied Solomon, "there's no time for detailed explanations at this juncture."

Goodchild turned to the projection on the holo-table. "Can you replay from four hours ago?" The projection flickered momentarily and was replaced with an almost identical view, except this time they could see several more craft in orbit around Europa.

"We announced our findings to all parties as soon as we had confirmation. Then we entered conclave and embarked on the delicate process of mediation." She paused for a moment and glanced over at the projection. "The Ceres frigate was first to respond, claiming that, in accordance with certain Outer Space Treaty amendments pertaining to salvage, they had legal rights. The Dyrell Labs ship countered this by claiming that it was their property to begin with and should be returned to them. Mars, on the other hand, makes no claim but refuses to allow either the Belt or Earth to take possession.

"Into this mix we, too, have laid a claim. Since the device was en route here, then here it should stay. The other craft in orbit made no claim, preferring instead to circle like vultures. This was the situation approximately four hours ago—until the Ceres frigate decided to take things into its own hands."

Goodchild paused for a moment then spoke a command for the projection to run forward in time.

"Stop. See the frigate?" she said, pointing at a bulky spaceship. As they watched, a small shuttle detached itself from the underside. "See, they are trying to land."

Goodchild made a hand gesture. "Play it forward."

The small shuttle dropped out of orbit and began to gently spiral down to the surface of Europa. It had reached around halfway in its decent when a speeding ball of plasma struck it from above. The craft was immediately encased in an incandescent mesh of electrical fuzz and began to spin wildly out of control. It fell rapidly, picking up speed as its engines failed to halt the downward acceleration. It finally impacted directly onto some domed facility at the periphery of the city in a fiery ball of rocket fuel.

"That crash must have been the tremor I felt when I woke up," said Miranda.

"Who attacked it?" said Scott.

"The Dyrell ship. But there's more," said Goodchild.

The projection ballooned out again, and they could see that a firefight had begun. The Ceres frigate was firing on the Dyrell ship, which returned fire and seem to strike a significant blow as the frigate began to move away and create some distance. A second barrage of plasma raked the frigate, and they could see it was breaking apart. Debris began to blossom out from several locations on its hull.

"This is crazy," said Scott. "Crazy."

Goodchild pointed at the Martian spacecraft. "Watch."

This ship had reoriented itself to be broadside of the

Dyrell craft, and like the great wooden warships of centuries past, opened up with a fusillade of fire. A second or two later the Dyrell ship returned fire, and soon the superiority of its weapons system overwhelmed its Martian opponent.

By now, all the other spacecraft in orbit were moving swiftly out of the way, powering their engines to move into higher and safer orbits. They had seen the weaponry at play and wanted no part of the fight.

Scott was transfixed by the plight of the Ceres craft. These were his people, his tribe. The craft, seeing itself out-gunned, had sought to accelerate out of range. It applied more power to its engines, and for a brief moment, it started to move away—just before it exploded.

Scott and the crew of the Hermes were speechless, watching in horror as the craft broke in two. Both sections dropped slowly out of orbit as the inevitable tug of Europa's gravity began to pull them downward. The projection followed their path as they fell lower and lower before finally crashing onto the surface some several kilometers away from the main center of population.

"Bastards," shouted Cyrus. "They can't get away with this—this is a declaration of war."

Scott looked over at Goodchild and just stared, hoping for the grand deacon to bring some rationality to what he had just witnessed.

"Your engineer is right. By their actions, they just

exported their war out into the solar system. This has been our fear all along, and now it has come to pass."

"Where are they now?" said Steph.

Goodchild again turned to the holo-table. "Bring us to real-time." The projection flickered, and they could now see just two ships in low orbit. "The Martian craft is crippled, but still retains enough integrity for life-support. The Dyrell craft is also damaged, but not to the same extent. The upshot is that they now control the space above us. They won the fight, and we are powerless to do anything."

"This is a crime. They have plunged us all into war," said Miranda.

"The repercussions of their action will play out across the system for decades to come," said Goodchild. "We are now at a nexus. A point at which, if we are not careful, the history of humanity as an inter-planetary species will enter a new phase. One of chaos, as each power seeks to gain dominion over the other."

"Bastards. They'll pay for this," said Cyrus.

"Your reaction is understandable. And it is emotions like these that will feed a war—one we feel is now inevitable."

Scott looked at two ships in orbit. The scars of battle could be seen on both, but it was the Martian craft that bore the brunt. Great gouges could be seen along its hull as it drifted in a small cloud of debris. Scott wondered if there might be bodies floating in that mass. "So much for mediation. What now?" said Scott.

"Ah, yes. Well... that's where you come in."

"Me?"

"I'm afraid so, Commander. Around twenty-five minutes ago, we received an ultimatum from the Dyrell craft. I think it might be best if you hear it for yourself." She pointed over at the holo-table.

The orbital projection flickered off and was replaced with a standard 2D screen projection, showing a simple head and shoulders image. It spoke.

"This is Commander Sorensen, of the Dyrell ship Enki. I'll be brief and to the point. You possess what rightfully belongs to us—and we want it back. You will also be aware by now that all other interested parties are... how shall I put it... no longer interested. So, you have two hours to deliver the EPR device back to us. You will utilize the lander from the Hermes to rendezvous with us where we can retrieve the device. Also, it has been requested that Commander Scott McNabb be the one to pilot the lander, since his family has a history of taking from Dyrell Labs things which don't belong to them. So, it is fitting he should be the one to follow in his father's footsteps.

"Failure to comply with this directive will result in the destruction of the facility housing the quantum intelligence, Solomon. To this end, we have already targeted the dome housing your QI. If we have not received the device within two hours of this message, we will destroy it. You have been warned."

The message ended, and the screen flickered off.

"Holy shit," said Cyrus.

"Scott, you don't need to do this," said Miranda.

"This is bullshit," said Steph.

Scott looked back at Goodchild. "There is no other choice, is there?"

The grand deacon shook her head. "We are powerless. All our efforts at communication have been met with silence."

"Why do you need to bring it to them? Why can't they just come down here a get it themselves?" said Miranda.

Solomon's voice then echoed out around the room. "They can't. We have detected damage to their shuttle. It is docked on the exterior of the craft and has been hit during the exchange of fire with the Ceres frigate. They can't land, so we must go to them."

"How much time have we got?"

"No, Scott. Don't do it. Don't give them the satisfaction. Let me go instead." Miranda gripped his arm and pulled him around.

"Yeah, screw them. We'll do it. You stay here," said Cyrus.

"No—I need to go. It's me they want."

"They're just trying to humiliate you, Scott," said Steph.

"I know. But what choice do we have?" He turned to face Goodchild again.

"This is not the outcome we had envisaged," said Goodchild. "In fact, it's the worst possible outcome."

"We shouldn't have come. All we've succeeded in doing is... starting a war," said Scott.

"War was coming long before this," said Goodchild. "If it had not started here, then it would start someplace else."

"What about the other craft? Will they help?" said Miranda.

"No. They are too afraid to take on Dyrell and too mistrusting of each other to band together."

"So, they will do nothing?"

Goodchild shook her head. "At best, they are simply observers. They will tell the story, nothing more."

"Well then, I better get going."

"No, wait," said Cyrus. "You're not doing this on your own."

Scott raised a palm. "I'll not put any more lives at risk. I need to do this myself."

"No way," said Miranda. "We're all in this together."

He sighed and shook his head slightly. "I really appreciate that, but too many have died already. You're safer here."

"Nonsense. We're coming with you." Steph was adamant.

"No. If you really want to help me, then listen to me: I want to do this alone. This is between me and Dyrell. Let me do what I have to do."

The crew were silent for a moment before Miranda spoke. "Okay, if you insist. But be careful and don't do anything stupid." She gave a light laugh. "Remember, I won't be there to protect you."

Scott gave a lopsided smile. "I'll keep it in mind."

"You best get going, Commander," said Goodchild. "The device will be brought to the landing pad, ready for you to take onboard your craft."

Scott nodded.

"They have given no clear directions after you take off, other than simply to rendezvous with the Dyrell ship. I presume they will give you more detailed instructions once you are on an approach vector."

"Okay, I need to go." He turned to the crew. "Come on. You can walk with me to the landing pad."

22

CHANGE OF PLAN

Scott strode down the wide corridor that led to the landing pad airlock. He had donned his EVA suit and carried his helmet under one arm. Regina Goodchild walked beside him, saying nothing. Behind him, Steph and Cyrus carried the EPR device, which had been reunited with its container. Miranda had chosen not to come. He was disappointed. Perhaps he had figured her wrong, like a lot of things in his life.

They arrived at the airlock and hit the button to open the inner door. Two drones now took the container from Steph and Cyrus.

"Time to go," said Scott as he held out a hand.

Cyrus took it, pulled him in, and embraced. "Good luck, buddy."

Scott nodded. "Thanks."

Steph then wrapped her arms around him.

"Hey," said Scott, "I'll be back."

Steph released him. "Sure. I know." She looked away.

The drones carried the container into the airlock, and Scott turned to walk in behind them.

"Wait, stop."

He looked back to see Miranda running up the corridor in a full EVA suit, in that long bounding style only possible in low gravity. She charged into the airlock beside him. "You're not going without me."

"But..."

"No buts, no arguments. I'm coming with you." She snapped on her helmet and elbowed him. "Better buckle up."

He had no choice, and no time to argue with her, so he just gave a smile. "Okay, if you insist." He got his helmet ready, closed the visor, and hit the button to close the inner door.

They walked out across the pad along with the two drones, carrying the container behind. Ahead was the lander, looking small and insignificant against the backdrop of the massive domes on either side and the expanse of space above.

"Why did you come? You know we probably won't be coming back," said Scott.

"Don't be such a pessimist. We're not going down without a fight. Anyway, they've nothing to gain by getting rid of us."

"Maybe, but don't you wonder why they're so keen to have me bring it?"

"They're just trying to rub it in, the whole family history thing, that's all."

"Why do you think I took this job? Five years in the backwaters of the Belt? I took it to get away from them. They were chasing me down for family debts. Debts supposedly owed to Dyrell. These are very nasty people."

"They don't care about that now. They just want this stupid thing." She pointed at the container the drones were carrying.

"I'm not so sure. The game is up for me—I don't see a way out of it."

"You can't just lay down and give up. You gotta stand up and fight."

"And where did fighting ever get you, Miranda?"

They stopped at the base of the lander, and Miranda turned to face him. "I don't need this shit from you right now, Scott. I'm trying to help you, in case you've forgotten. I'm putting my ass on the line here, so let's just get this done, and go home. Okay?"

"Sorry. Forget I said that. I... I'm really glad you're here."

Miranda sighed. "Come on, let's get this thing on board and get moving—before I change my mind."

A few moments later, they were both strapped into their seats inside the lander cockpit. Miranda busied herself powering up the systems and doing a pre-flight check.

"So, what's the plan?" she said as she glanced over at him.

"We don't want to get too close to the Dyrell ship. So, I suggest we get to within a reasonable distance and shove this container out of the lander into space—in their general direction, of course. They can go and pick it up themselves."

"Okay. Let's do it, then."

The craft's engines ignited and Miranda gently piloted it up off the pad. Through the main window, Scott could see the massive domes of Europa scroll down and across as the craft lifted and rotated out of the landing area.

The had only risen a few hundred meters when the comms bursts to life. "Europa craft, this is the Dyrell ship Enki. Please rendezvous at our stern port-side airlock where you can dock and transfer the cargo. Over."

Scott was about to transmit a reply when Miranda stopped him. "Wait. That's not going to work."

"I know, not our plan."

"No, I don't mean that. I mean they obviously don't realize just how old this machine is. It has no universal docking port. We are technically incapable of docking with the Dyrell ship."

"Okay, well that solves that problem." Scott hit the transmit button on the comms desk. "Enki, this is Europa Craft. We do not have a universal docking port so are unable to comply. However, we will bring our craft close to your stern port and jettison the cargo. You can pick it up by EVA. Over."

There was a momentary pause as Scott and Miranda exchanged glances.

"This is not acceptable. Please standby and await updated instructions. Out."

"I knew it," said Scott. "They won't be satisfied until they get me onboard that ship."

"Screw them. We just stick to our own plan."

"How badly do they want me? That's the question. Badly enough to start taking potshots at Europa if I don't comply? I would be putting other people at risk. I can't do that."

Miranda said nothing, just glanced over at him with a concerned look on her face.

"Wait a minute," said Scott. "That shuttle we took from Neo City, it has a universal docking port?"

"Well, yeah. But I don't see how that helps," said Miranda.

Scott leaned in again and hit the transmit button. "Enki, this is Europa Craft. Change of plan. We are redirecting to the Hermes and transferring cargo onto a shuttle that will be able to dock with your craft. Over."

"What the hell are you doing? Are you mad?" Miranda reached over and grabbed Scott's arm.

"Remember what you said? Sometimes you gotta stand up and fight."

"Yeah, but this is just playing right into their hands, Scott."

"You're forgetting: that shuttle is not the only thing sitting in the hangar."

Miranda gave him a strange look, trying to figure out what he meant. He was surprised she didn't get it, so he leaned over and put his hand on her arm. "Trust me."

"Europa Craft, this is Enki. Your amended plan is acceptable. You have thirty minutes to execute, or we will commence firing on Europa. Out."

"Bastards," said Miranda, before changing flight direction. "I hope to hell you know what you're doing, Scott. So, what's in the hangar that's going to help us get out of this one?"

"High explosives," said Scott.

"Of course." A big smile radiated across her face. "Now you're talking my kinda language."

Scott hit transmit again, but this time it was to contact the Hermes. "Aria, this is Commander McNabb. Can you open the hangar bay doors? We're coming in. Over."

"Ah, Scott. Good to hear your voice. I have been very concerned for you all. Is everyone okay? Over."

"Yes, all good. Out."

Miranda was now pushing the little lander as fast as she dared to get to the Hermes with enough time to make the transfer. Ahead, they could see the old space station coming into view, its hangar doors already open.

"Any ideas on how we're going to work this?" said Miranda.

"Once we're back on board, we can have Aria get the code to open the container from Solomon. Then fill it with explosives and deliver it."

"I get that, but how do we get away if we're docked to the Enki?"

"We wing it."

"Wing it?"

"Let's not worry about it now—let's just get the first part done."

Miranda deftly brought the craft in to land on the extended platform. They felt a slight jolt on touchdown as clamps swiveled over to secure it in place. The platform started to retract back into the hangar. A moment later, the bay doors closed and Scott and Miranda began to unload the container.

They strapped it down to the floor of the hangar so it wouldn't float off in the zero-gee environment, and Scott entered the code that Solomon had given them to open it. Miranda already had the container with the explosives open. "Any idea how these work?" She picked out one of the small cylinders.

"They're standard issue for asteroid mining." Scott moved over beside her and lifted out one of the small handheld remote detonators.

"There's a number on the side of each cylinder. Simply tap it into the keypad on the detonator and it's primed." He flicked open a red cover on the side. "Once it's active, press here and... ker-boom." He looked into the box of explosives. "There's enough here to turn an M-Class asteroid into ball bearings. So, we'll only need a few to put a great big hole in the Dyrell ship." He began transferring some of the cylinders over to the container, one by one.

"Okay, that should be more than enough. Let's get it onboard, and I can arm them en route."

They spent a few more minutes getting it transferred onto the shuttle and Scott started arming the detonator as Miranda powered up the craft and ran through the pre-flight checks. "We still don't have a plan for how to do this and get away."

"I was thinking," Scott looked over at her with a smile, "weapons would be good. Where are the ones we brought back from Neo City?"

"I stashed them in Cyrus's workshop."

"I think you should go get them."

"Do we have time?"

"Yes, now go. I still need to prime the rest of these explosives."

Miranda hesitated for a beat before rising from her seat and clambering out of the craft. Scott watched her float across the hangar space and into the interior airlock. Once she was out of sight, he sat down in the pilot seat and hit the comms on his headset. "Aria, open the hangar bay doors."

"Yes, Commander."

Scott took a few moments to familiarize himself with the layout of the flight console of the shuttle. He had flown a few of these shuttles before but it was a long time ago, and he was a bit rusty.

"Aria, extend the platform, please."

"Should you not wait for Miranda to return?"

"Just do it, Aria."

"As you wish, Commander."

He felt a judder as the floor below the craft started to extend outward. His comms burst into life. "Scott, what are you doing?" It was Miranda. She would be unable to enter the hangar now that the bay doors were open and the platform moving.

"I'm sorry, Miranda. But there is no way out of this. I have to do it alone."

"No, Scott, we're in this together. Don't do it."

"There's no need for both of us to die."

"Scott."

"You were right, Miranda. It's time for me to stand up and fight back."

"Scott, no."

He switched the comms unit off and powered away from the Hermes.

23

DYRELL

Scott took it slow, no need to rush. He felt a deep calm envelop him; he knew what he needed to do, and it felt right. He was more certain of this path than any other he had ever embarked on, and with it came a transcendent clarity—a purity that he now understood. It was straight, and true, and final.

For too long, his life had been defined by the actions of others. It had molded him more than he had realized. Central to this had been witnessing the utter futility of his father's battle for truth and justice, which ultimately killed him and instilled in Scott an almost visceral desire to not follow the same failed path. His father's philosophy had been one of direct confrontation to the point of destruction of almost all that he had held dear. So, Scott's would be the opposite. If his father's belief was fight, then his would be flight. And so he had run far away from Earth and the ruins of his father's intransigence. But, as it turned out, far away was not far enough. Dyrell were not content with the price they had already extracted—they wanted more. So, Scott ran further, out to the very edges of the Belt. But even in that remote corner of the solar system, he still could not hide from the fickleness of chance. It was as if his destiny was to be forever embroiled with the actions of the past.

Yet sitting here now, in this shuttle, on this mission, he could not help feeling that there was a little part of his father riding with him, entangled within the quantum device he now carried. It seemed fitting for him to think this way. They were in it together. They would make it all right again, exact a just revenge. Together, they would ride this steely chariot into the gates of hell and annihilate all before them in a fireball of retribution.

The comms burst into life.

"Scott?"

"Miranda?" How was she communicating? Then he realized he had only switched off their suit comms; she was now using ship-to-ship. "You need to get off this channel—they can hear."

"It's encrypted, Scott. Only we can hear."

He reached over to switch it off, but hesitated.

"Don't do this, Scott. There is a better way." Her voice was stressed, her words rushed.

"It's okay, Miranda. I'm here with my father. We're doing it together."

"Your father?"

"Yes. We're going to charge straight in through their front door and put it all to right."

"Scott, you don't have to do it this way." Her tone was more measured now.

Through the shuttle window, Scott saw the Dyrell craft getting closer. Time to step on the gas.

"Time to go, Miranda."

"No, wait, wait. Aria says there might be another way."

"Thanks for thinking about me, but the time is now."

"No, Scott..."

He switched off the comms.

She was distracting him from the mission, making him lose focus. He needed to concentrate, find his mark, and aim for it.

What did she mean by "another way?" he thought. Don't go there. Focus. He fought to keep his mind on track. But the thought would not go away now that Miranda had planted the seed.

Destroying the device was easy. Simply press the button on the detonator he had clipped to his EVA suit. But to destroy the Dyrell ship, he would have to get the container inside, although that was not difficult either. If he were to actually dock with the Dyrell, the doors would open and they would simply take it inside themselves. The problem with that, though, was would he get time to detonate it before they figured out what he was doing? Possible, he thought. He would still be able to realize his objective. Of course, he would be blown to smithereens.

But that was okay, too as he had already reconciled himself to that.

So, what did Miranda mean? How was there another way? The thought would not leave him, and he was getting close to the Dyrell ship. He would need to make his mind up soon or lose the opportunity.

The way Scott saw it, there was no way in which he could get the container inside the ship, undock the shuttle, and then detonate it from a safe distance. The problem was once the shuttle connected, it could only be released by the Dyrell ship. Scott would be stuck there.

"Think," he said out loud. Maybe I could blow out the docking port? After all, he had a container load of explosives. All he needed was one charge for the port. There would be more than enough left to convert the Dyrell into scrap metal. But he only had one detonator. Unless...

Scott slowed the craft down so he could buy more time, and unstrapped himself from the pilot seat. He floated over to where the container with the EPR device was tied down and opened the lid. Inside, he had stuffed around twenty of the explosive canisters. He picked one out and examined it for a moment, put it back, and picked out another one. He was looking for a particular type, one with a built-in timer. He was pretty sure there would be at least one in here. The container these had come from was standard issue, so there should be both timed and remote-detonated charges in the mix.

On the third try, he found one. He stuffed it into a

pocket, closed the lid of the container, and moved back to his seat. On the primary cockpit screen, proximity detectors were picking up the docking beacon of the Dyrell ship.

It's now or never, he thought. Time to decide. Scott paused for a beat then leaned over and flicked a switch to allow the Dyrell ship to take control and adjust the shuttle's orientation to line it up on the docking port. The monitor bleeped as the craft drew closer. Finally, Scott felt the thud as the two ships made contact and locking bolts fired to clamp him in place. He was now immobile, and would remain so until the mothership released him or he somehow broke free.

He didn't have much time; they would be opening the docking hatch in a minute or two. He rose from the pilot seat and floated into the cargo area of the shuttle. He untied the container with the EPR device and moved both it and himself into a position directly opposite the hatch. There was no airlock on the shuttle side, but there would be on the mothership. Therefore, he had to clear that to have any chance of his crazy plan succeeding. He tethered himself to the floor of the cargo hold, psyched himself up, and waited.

Scott felt, rather than heard, the clunking of the outer airlock door being opened. He wound himself up, ready to spring. The inner shuttle hatch finally swung open, revealing three figures on the far side, two holding plasma guns. Scott pushed the container out toward the opening with all the speed and strength he could muster.

The container shot forward and crashed into the three figures, carrying them along as it plowed on into the cargo hold beyond.

Scott was snapped back by the tether he had attached to the hull of the shuttle. He undid the clasp and made his way through the hatch opening and into the airlock of the Dyrell ship. He saw that the container was still moving across the big internal cargo hold, as the three figures tumbled and flailed about, trying to find purchase on something to get them reoriented.

He moved over to the inner door and hit the button to close it just as a bolt from a plasma gun blasted into the side wall. It crackled and fizzled, and he could smell the tang of ozone in the air. He finally got the door shut and wondered if there was some way that he could jam it closed. But nothing came to mind, so he left it and turned his attention to locating the control box for the locking clamps on the outer hull. He spotted it straightaway and moved over beside it, taking the charge from his pocket as he went. He set the timer for twenty seconds and wedged in beside the control box.

Scott moved back into the shuttle and closed the hatch door, spinning the wheel to lock it shut. Then, in one quick move, he pushed off and flew back through to the cockpit, closing the bulkhead door that separated this area from the cargo hold. It was built for strength and would offer him some protection from the blast. Once that happened, the shuttle would lose atmosphere, so he snapped on his EVA suit helmet, booted it up, and strapped himself in.

When the charge finally detonated, Scott was slammed sideways with the force and whacked his head hard against the inside of his helmet. Lights and alerts flashed all across the flight deck as the shuttle went into cardiac arrest. The stars outside scrolled across his field of vision and the shuttle was hurled outward. There was another violent judder, and the shuttle swung back. Shit, he thought, it's still attached. It didn't work.

The craft again slammed off the hull of the Dyrell. Something still held it, but only just. Scott reached for the controls, hoping against hope that the engines would work. The craft powered up as he pushed forward on the controls for maximum thrust. But he was going nowhere, at least not relative to the Dyrell. Then the power cut and the cockpit descended into darkness. Fuck. he slammed his fists on the console in frustration.

After a moment, Scott regained his composure and calmly sat back in the seat. "Well, at least I gave it a try," he said to himself as he reached for the remote detonator still strapped to his EVA suit—and pressed the button.

24

DEBRIS FIELD

Miranda tried several times to regain contact with Scott after he had switched off his comms. Why was he doing this? she wondered. Why this crazy suicide run? All he had to do to destroy the device was to float it out into space and blow it up. Why kill himself in the process. Has he completely flipped?

"Scott, talk to me," she tried yet again.

"He is not going to respond," said Aria.

"How do you know?"

"Voice analysis of his last conversation indicates a primary resolve—not easy to overturn."

Miranda sighed and sat back. The QI was probably right. There was nothing more she could do except watch his destruction on the main monitor. She glanced up and zoomed in on the shuttle. She had imagined he would start to pick up speed so he could ram the Dyrell at maximum velocity but, so far, he had maintained his slow, steady pace. Miranda watched for a while as the gap between the shuttle and the Dyrell closed, and still he maintained the same speed. In fact, it seemed like he was slowing down. Then, at the last minute, he started to speed up. Miranda was sure this was it: he was going to ram straight into the hull of the Dyrell. She was standing now; her hands gripped the edge of the bridge console as she watched. But he didn't.

Instead, he brought the shuttle in slowly and docked. Miranda sat back down and breathed a sigh of relief.

"Looks like he's decided not to kill himself after all."

"Not yet," said Aria.

"Can you zoom in more on the ship, Aria?"

"Certainly." The screen filled now with an image of the shuttle docked with the Dyrell.

"I wonder what he's doing?" Miranda's question was answered almost immediately. An explosion at the docking port seemed to hinge the shuttle away from the mothership and debris shot out into space. "He's blown the airlock." She jumped up. "Come on Scott, get away, get moving."

The shuttle engines powered up, and she realized something was still holding it to the Dyrell. It then seemed to lose power and crash back down, slamming against the hull. The nose of the shuttle bounced and then something somewhere broke as the rear end rose up and tumbled forward. It started to float free, just as the entire middle section of the Dyrell ship was ripped apart in a massive explosion. An enormous fiery ball blossomed out and seemed to engulf the entire craft, and from its core, a cloud of debris ballooned out.

"Oh my god, he's done it, he's blown it up."

The inferno at its center quickly extinguished as all the oxygen in the Dyrell was consumed. Miranda saw a gap widen where the ship had broken apart, disgorging a sea of wreckage.

"Can you see the shuttle, Aria? Is there anything left of it?"

"I'm switching to hyperspectral." The monitor now filled with a multitude of garishly colored blooms overlaid with a fine grid pattern. Several cross-hair targets danced about the screen momentarily before finally stabilizing on two small patches of color.

"I have located two major components of the shuttle. Resolving back to visual, and tracking."

The monitor returned to a true image with the targets still visible and tracking the outward trajectory of the tagged components. The image zoomed more in as it tracked a blurry smudge. "This section consists of the main engine compartment."

The screen monetarily zoomed out and shifted focus to the second larger, blurry image. "This looks to be the cockpit section."

"Is it intact?"

"I'm not sure what you mean by intact."

"Could Scott have survived?"

"If the rear bulkhead held, then theoretically it's possible. Although it's highly unlikely."

Miranda watched as the remains of the shuttle spiraled out from the epicenter of the blast and drifted into space. "We need to go after him." She sat down again and started plotting a course.

"We don't have the fuel, Miranda. We used everything we had in getting to Europa. We're simply using the plasma drive to keep us in orbit, and it doesn't have the thrust we need to intercept. We could eventually catch up with it. But I calculate that wouldn't be for at least three days."

"What about the lander?"

"Yes, it's possible. In fact, it may be your only chance of intercepting it."

"Okay, get it ready, Aria. I'm going after him."

"The trajectory of that object is such that you will only have one point of interception. If you miss it, Miranda, it will be very difficult for you to catch it again."

"I'll get it. Don't worry." She ran out of the bridge, took the step lift down one of the central spokes, and moved as fast as she could to the hangar. Aria's probably right, she thought: Scott's dead. But she had to try. Even if there was only a slim possibility—she had to try.

As Miranda entered the hangar, an alert started blaring out of the PA. "What's going on, Aria?"

"Proximity alert. We have debris from the explosion heading our way. I will try to maneuver the Hermes as best I can to minimize any impact damage. But you will need to be careful out there. The bulk of the fragments will begin passing in three minutes. Some have enough velocity to puncture the lander's hull."

"Okay. I get the picture." She had suited up in the airlock and was now climbing into the lander's cockpit. She handed over flight control to Aria as it was tracking the shuttle and would keep her on the best course for an intercept. All she had to do was sit tight and hope she wasn't hit by anything. She kept the internal cabin depressurized as this would mitigate any minor punctures. With no atmosphere inside the lander, it wouldn't suddenly decompress if it got hit. But her EVA suit was another matter. It would be the only thing keeping her alive out there.

"Okay, Aria. Ready."

The hangar bay doors opened, and the craft started to move out on its platform. Within a minute, it was taking off and banking away from the Hermes. On the primary monitor, Miranda watched the blip that represented the remains of Scott's shuttle. She was slammed back into her seat as the lander throttled up to full power. Aria's voice echoed in her helmet. "Micro debris incoming in twenty-eight seconds."

Miranda gripped the armrests tight and tried to breathe normally. Alerts flashed up on screen as the hull was peppered with shrapnel. A tiny hole suddenly appeared in the hull, just above her head, then another, and another—and these were just the ones she could see. The little lander was being turned into a colander. Flight controls flickered momentarily before they finally went dark.

Holy crap, she thought.

"Miranda, are you okay?"

"Sort of. Console is dead though."

"The debris cloud has passed now. I can try to instigate a reboot." The console flickered momentarily and then lit up again.

"It's back," she shouted. "It's back."

"The craft has suffered damage to the control systems. I've managed to get power back up, but I can't say for how long."

"How bad?"

"You don't have much time. The systems could fail again and I may not be able to restore them remotely."

"Okay."

Miranda glanced at the monitor. The blip was much closer now. She looked out the window, trying to get a visual. "I don't see it, Aria."

"It should be above you."

She craned her neck and scanned the black empty space above the craft. Something flashed. She studied it and realized it was the shuttle, spinning gently, the brilliant light from Jupiter reflected off what was left of its forward windows.

"Got it, Aria."

"I'll bring you as close I can. The rest will be up to you."

Miranda undid the restraining straps on the pilot seat

and floated over to the main hatch. Beside it, hung midway up the inner wall, was mounted a thruster pack. She maneuvered her back into the harness and secured it to her EVA suit. She reached over and hit the button to open the hatch.

Outside, the vast, stormy surface of Jupiter dominated the view. Silhouetted against it was the slowly spinning remains of the shuttle cockpit. The small craft had been torn asunder by the explosion. But the cockpit section had remained relatively intact since it was designed to withstand greater impacts than the rest of the ship. Nonetheless, as the wreckage tumbled, Miranda saw it was seriously banged up. The roof and sides had long rents and gouges in the metal. The front windows were cracked and splintered. Her heart sank at the sight. Could anyone have survived that? she wondered.

"That's as close as I can safely bring you, Miranda," Aria's voice resonated in her helmet.

"Okay, I'm going to take a look." She clipped a tether to her suit and then thought better of it. It would keep her attached to the lander, but since the wreckage was tumbling, she might end up getting it wrapped around it, and that would be catastrophic. So, she unclipped it, and checked the thruster pack for power. "Okay, here goes."

Miranda pushed herself out the open hatch in the direction of the spinning carcass, touching lightly on the thruster controls to slow herself down and not bounce off if she came in too quick. She tried to align herself with the center of spin, but it seemed to be rotating on several axes. Aiming as best she could, Miranda tried to grab hold of the slowest moving section, which was the front window. She bounced off on her first attempt but managed to find a grip on the second try.

The quartz glass on this section of the window was still intact even though it had numerous deep gouges in it. It was also blackened to the point where Miranda had difficulty seeing through it. She moved slowly, hand over hand, across what was left of the front of the craft to the left-hand side window. This had shattered completely, and she was able to poke her head in and inspect the cockpit.

On the far side, the motionless body of Commander Scott McNabb was still strapped into the pilot's seat. His head was slumped forward, and his arms were suspended limply by his sides. In front of him floated the detonator, still tethered to his suit.

"Scott," said Miranda, as if he would somehow miraculously hear her and make some response.

She examined the gap in the window and realized she would not be able to fit through with the bulky thruster pack attached. She considered taking it off, but that might be risky: if she were to lose her grip on the wreckage, then she would have no way of getting back to the lander. She decided instead to check out the rest of the hull to see if there was a gap big enough for her to fit through.

She spent a few minutes traversing the hull of the shattered craft. It was pockmarked with impacts, and here and there it bore the signs of deeper traumas. But it seemed to have stood up remarkably well. But nowhere was there a tear or gap that she could utilize. Even the rear cockpit bulkhead had not broken. It had taken a considerable blast as the entire section was now concave. She tried the door, but it was too bent and buckled to move. She had no option but to try squeeze in through the front window.

Miranda worked her way back to the nose of the craft. After a few more minutes, she had taken off the bulky thruster pack and tethered it to the hull as best she could. It was difficult as she had to do it one-handed. With the other, she made sure she had a good grip on the craft. Eventually, she began to push herself through the broken window, twisting and tugging until finally she was inside the cockpit.

She floated over to where Scott was strapped in. Blood streaked down the inside of his helmet visor, and as she moved closer, she saw his eyes were closed and his face a bloodied mess. She couldn't tell if he was dead or alive, so she checked the readouts on his wrist control pad. The suit still had power and at least two more hours of breathable air. This meant it was also still intact and able to retain one atmosphere of pressure. Her heart skipped a beat at the realization that maybe, just maybe, he might still be alive.

Miranda undid his harness and pulled him up out of the seat. After several minutes of careful maneuvering, she had managed to get herself back outside and had most of Scott's limp body pulled through. But something was catching. She pushed him back in a little to see what it was. A section of the thick broken window jutted out. There was no way she could break it, so she had no choice but to try to pull him through, even though she risked damaging the integrity of his EVA suit. She braced her feet against the hull and pulled at him with all her strength.

He broke free with a suddenness that gave Miranda no time to react. She found herself tumbling backwards off the hull and into space, still clutching Scott's limp body. She saw the thruster pack still tethered to the hull of the shuttle which they were now drifting slowly away from. Oh shit, she thought, as the dire situation she now found herself in dawned on her. Without the thruster, she had no way to maneuver, no way to return to the lander. She was drifting free in space. Like a beached whale or an upturned turtle, she could flail her limbs around all she liked—it wasn't going to do a damn thing. But it wasn't time to panic just yet.

"Aria, I have a problem."

Silence.

"Aria, can you hear me?"

Silence.

"Aria, come in. I could really do with some help here."

But there was no reply forthcoming, just a low background static echoing in her helmet.

"ARIA?"

Nothing.

By now, a sense of panic was beginning to well up from deep within her. She fought to control it. Her suit comms must have been damaged in the debris strike. "Think, goddamnit." She looked around and already both the wreck of the shuttle and the Hermes lander were quite a distance away. At that moment, she realized there was nothing she could do. She had blown it.

She gazed at Scott's bloodied face through the helmet visor. "I'm sorry, Scott. I've screwed up again. I always end up doing something stupid, don't I?" She leaned her head in so their visors touched, and she thought she caught a flicker of his eyelids. He was still alive, but for how much longer?

"I never seem to get things right, Scott. It's the story of my life." She glanced over in the direction of the lander, only to see it receding further and further away. "Well, here we are, at the end of the line. No way out of this one, Commander. No way home." She looked back again at the broken and bloodied face of Scott McNabb. "I'm sorry I couldn't save you. I tried, I really did."

After a few moments, Miranda checked her own oxygen supply. She had just under four hours. Four hours to live, she thought, unless she could think of something or her comms started working again.

"Air," she shouted into her helmet. "Of course. Why didn't I think of it before? Maybe there is a way."

She had remembered a last-ditch action from training, one you only do if there was absolutely no other option. "Hang in there, Scott. We may have a chance after all." She clipped his EVA suit to hers with a short tether, and then started searching in the cargo pocket on her right thigh. She pulled out a short knife with a serrated blade and sharp point, and gripped it firmly in one hand. Okay, here goes. I hope to hell this works. She opened the palm of her left hand and gently twisted the point of the knife in through the glove.

When it finally punctured, the result was chaotic. Air spewed out and swung her arm back with a force she wasn't expecting. They began to spin around and around before Miranda had time to react. She closed her fist to slow the escaping air and tried to figure out their orientation. But it was difficult to see anything other than the sweep of the gas giant Jupiter flash past. She adjusted the position of her palm in the opposite direction to their spin and slowly opened her fist. Air hissed out again and started to counter her spin, slowing her down.

After a few more attempts, Miranda felt she had some measure of control even though it was still wild and lacked any finesse. Nonetheless, she managed to sight the wrecked shuttle far off in the distance, visible only by the flash of reflected light from its broken windows. Beside it, the lander still waited. By adjusting the orientation of her hand, and by opening and closing her fist, she managed to get them moving in the right direction. A sense of hope returned to her. "Hold on, Scott. We're not dead yet."

She came in way too fast on her first attempt and missed the lander by several meters. It took her a frustratingly long time to get them both reoriented back in the right direction, but she took it slower this time, and she was beginning to get the feel for the physics of her rudimentary thruster. It took her three more attempts before she finally slammed into the side of the lander. She scrabbled frantically for a hand hold, but Scott's limp body was getting in the way, and she failed to find purchase. They bounced off again. Dammit! Miranda was getting frustrated and began to worry that her air supply would run out, now that she was using it as a propellant.

She was coming in slow and controlled on her seventh attempt when the low air alert finally flashed on her helmet screen. She glanced at it. Twenty-five minutes left. That was breathable air, but at the rate she was expending it out of her suit, the reality was much less. "Just stay focused," she said to herself. "Keep your eyes on the prize."

The lander slowly came toward her. Miranda targeted a group of handles surrounding the hatch. Any of them would do, she wasn't fussy. But she could only grab it with one hand; opening the fist on the other would just send her spiraling off course again. She had readjusted the harness attaching Scott to her EVA suit so that he floated behind her. Her incoming vector was true, and Miranda managed to grab the handle on her first attempt. She gripped it tight and breathed a long, slow sigh of relief. She hung there for a second or two just gathering herself together, before finally reaching over and opening the hatch to the lander. Miranda maneuvered herself inside, pulling Scott through behind her.

The cockpit was dark. No power.

"Aria?" she ventured a call, but there was still no response. Her helmet screen flashed eleven minutes.

"Reboot. Try to reboot the power," she said to herself as she rummaged in a pocket and pulled out an EVA suit patch. It should stem the leak and mean she wouldn't be trying to work one-handed. She lost a few more valuable minutes of air in the process. Ordinarily she would simply pressurize the cockpit, but there was no point since the lander had been shot through with microdebris.

She maneuvered Scott into a seat and strapped him in. Only then did Miranda finally try a system reboot. She flicked off all the power switches and then started switching them back on again in sequence. The cockpit console lit up like a festival.

Miranda dived into the pilot seat and hit the ignition. The craft rumbled and the engines fired. She looked over at Scott, his head slumped down to his chest. "Going home, buddy. Going home."

With her suit comms shot and no way to contact Aria, she prayed that it had the good sense to leave the hangar bay doors open. Her helmet screen flashed three minutes in bright red numbers.

The bay doors were open, but there was no time to celebrate. Miranda had decided not to land on the extended platform and wait until it slowly retracted inside. There was no time for that—she would just fly it straight in, and to hell with the damage. She lined up on the opening and nosed the craft as gently as she could in through the gap. It banged off the ceiling. She cut the power, and it landed hard on the floor. Her helmet screeched a critical low oxygen alert; she was running on empty. She took a deep breath and held it. This might be my last, she thought.

Miranda unfastened Scott, dragged him out of the lander, and pushed off for the internal airlock on the far side of the hangar. Her lungs began to hurt as she flung him in. She hit pressurize, the outer door closed, and the internal space hissed and spat as jets of air filled its interior... 10%, 20%. The airlock display ticked up slowly and the pressure increased. Come on, come on. She fought the desire to breathe in, knowing there was nothing left in her tank. The green alert flashed on the airlock monitor and Miranda snapped off her helmet and took a long gasp of air.

"Miranda, are you okay? What happened?" Aria's voice broke in.

Miranda waved a weary hand in the air as she breathed deeply a few times. "Suit comms shot... lost my grip on the shuttle... long story."

"You successfully retrieved the commander, I see. Is he still alive?"

"I don't know. I'm checking now." She floated over to him and gently removed his helmet to reveal a bloodied head. She held her hand up to her mouth to stifle her shock. Yet on closer inspection, it looked worse than it actually was. Very tentatively, she reached over and pressed the back of her hand to his cheek. His skin was warm. "I think he's still alive, but only just."

She held his head in her hands and looked at his broken face. "Hang in there, you crazy bastard. Don't die on me now." She pulled him to her, opened the interior airlock door, and started making her way to medbay.

25

RETURN TO THE STARS

The remaining crew of the Hermes gathered on either side of the body, along with several representatives from Europa. It rested on a low pallet and had been bound in a simple white sheet. At its head, a priestly figure stood, raised a hand to quieten the assembled group, and began to speak.

"Forged in the cauldron of the stars and wrought from the cosmos, we are the creation of the celestial heavens. As a star dies, it offers forth its life-forming matter into the universe so we can exist. Its death is our life. So, let the cosmos now reclaim, and gather unto itself our fallen comrade, Rick Marentz. And so from whence you came, so shall you return, back to the stars, back into the cradle of the universe."

The figure now signaled to the assembled mourners that they may proceed. Scott nodded in return and placed a hand on one side of the pallet where the remains of his friend and colleague had been laid to rest. The other crew of the Hermes moved forward, placing hands on the pallet, and together they pushed the body out through the open hangar bay doors.

They all stood there for a while, watching as the body of the old miner drifted out into space. A tear formed in Scott's left eye; his right eye was still bandaged. He moved his hand reflexively to wipe it away, only to remember that he, like the others, was encased in an EVA suit. He lowered his head instead and let the tear fall to the inside of his visor. After a moment, he took one last look out the bay doors at the body of his dear friend. He could just pick it out in the vastness, slowly tumbling on its way into the void. He turned around and moved back to the hangar airlock.

~

ONCE BACK IN the pressurized environment of the Hermes, he sat down, removed his EVA suit helmet, and wiped his eye with the back of his hand. He had a strong urge to scratch the bandage over his right eye, but he had been warned not to by the surgeons on Europa, who had done such an excellent job of sticking him back together. He might regain the sight in that eye as long as he refrained from scratching it. So, he resisted the urge and instead felt down along the side of his jaw. The pain was growing less and less each day, and soon they could take the wire out. He had taken a risk putting on an EVA suit, as any urge to throw up could be disastrous with a wired jaw. Nevertheless, he was determined to do it for his old friend.

He had been lucky, so they said. The shuttle had a reinforced cockpit design and so managed to stay relatively intact in the blast that had ripped apart the Dyrell ship. His lower body sustained a few cracked ribs and a lot of bruising. But his main injuries were inflicted when his head slammed against the side of his helmet. Luckily it was only his jaw that broke and not the helmet. Yet in the end, his continued existence in the solar system was down to Miranda risking her own life to save him from his reckless stupidity. Her words, not his.

He had been prepared to die. He had resigned himself to that fate, had accepted it, even embraced it. Now though, he was on the mend both physically and mentally. A new appreciation for life grew inside of him. Miranda's actions had given him a second chance, and he felt he owed her somehow for the gift she had bestowed upon him. It was partly a burden, a responsibility not to waste this chance, and partly a release from the shackles of his own disengagement from life. He was born anew, and he would never be the same again.

The funeral party all migrated out from the hangar of the Hermes and down to the comfort of the canteen. Along with the crew, they had been joined by some officials from Europa, people they had come to know since the ending of hostilities. Scott had assumed that they would be no longer welcome here since they were responsible for bringing death and destruction raining down on what was a peaceful and harmonious society. But this was not the case. In fact, far from it: the council of Europa seemed to welcome them even more, regarding them as saviors of the peace. Particularly Scott for his almost-ultimate sacrifice in destroying the device once and for all. They viewed it as a selfless, noble act, one worthy of their admiration and respect. They had even dispatched a crew to patch up their ship and resupply it. Yet, Scott had to admit, he was not looking forward to returning to Ceres. However, they were in no hurry.

Cyrus had just cracked open a bottle of whiskey that they had found stashed in Rick's cabin. It was old and of fine quality, meaning it was expensive and well beyond Rick's pay grade. How he came to possess such an item was the source of much speculation. Cyrus charged their glasses and Scott took his cue to raise his to all assembled. "To Rick," he said as raised his glass. It was as much as he was willing—or able—to say through his wired jaw and welling emotions.

They all clinked and sipped, and slowly they began to recount tales of Rick's past adventures. Some fact, some myth, but mostly legend. Cyrus had just launched into recounting a story of the time Rick and two miners were trapped on an asteroid after they accidentally blew a hole in their lander. They managed to survive for seven days cooped up in an emergency shelter before being picked up by a passing frigate. The story mainly centered around how one of the miners became demented and tried to kill Rick, convinced that he was a flesh-eating, alien monster. Scott had heard it many times before so he shuffled off to the side of the group and sat down to spend some quiet time with his thoughts.

After a while, Miranda wandered over to him and sat down. "So how are you holding up?"

Scott cast her a sideways glance. "Physically or mentally?"

Miranda gave a light laugh. "Both, I suppose."

"Physically, I'm all beat up. There isn't a section of my body that doesn't have pain. But, hey... I'll get over it, in time." He raised his glass to her. They clinked.

"So, mentally?"

"Ah... well, sad to be leaving Rick behind." He glanced out through the wide canteen window at the stars beyond, perhaps hoping to catch a glimpse of his old friend tumbling into infinity. "And sad to be leaving here. I'm just getting to like it." He paused for a moment and looked into his glass. "Have you thought about what you're going to do when we get back to Ceres?"

Miranda sighed. "I don't know. Find another job I guess, now that the rest of the survey mission is canceled."

"It was canceled the moment we found that derelict ship. The only difference was we thought we would all be in for a big payday. Now it's back to working for a living again."

"Yeah, and it isn't going to get any easier since we've

made a lot of enemies during this escapade. It's going to be hard to pick up the pieces."

Scott looked over at the group from Europa. They were being entertained by some of Steph's tales of Rick's exploits. "We've made a few new ones, though."

"I'm going to miss this place, too. I hate to admit it, but I could get quite comfortable here."

"Really?" Scott cocked an eyebrow at her. "I didn't think this sort of pacifist, quasi-spiritual culture was your sort of thing."

Miranda smiled. "Neither did I until I spent some time here. Granted, it takes a bit of getting used to, but it's nice to feel like you're not just being used as a tool in someone else's game plan." She leaned in a little. "You know, I spent years fighting other people's wars. A pawn to be shoved around at someone else's whim. And then, when you're no use, they just drop you. I get the impression that doesn't happen around here."

Scott gave a light laugh. "Am I really hearing this? You're going all warm and fuzzy on me, just when I started getting the fighting bug." He looked out the window again. "I can't say that being nice ever did me any good."

"That's because you were being a doormat, Scott, letting everybody wipe their feet on you."

Scott gave her an insulted look. "Thanks."

"Well, you were. As well as being totally disconnected from everything around you."

"You sure know how to make a guy feel good,

Miranda. Do yourself a favor and don't take up a career in diplomacy."

"Just saying. I mean, it makes what you did so... incredible. I don't know if I could have done it."

"Yeah, you would. You just never found something you really believed in. Fighting was a job for you. You did it with your head, not your heart."

She gave him a look. "I'm not sure how to take that. If I was just using my head, I would never have tried to save you."

Scott looked back at her and smiled. "Well, I for one am very glad you did."

She reached over, wrapped an arm around his shoulder, and gave him a kiss on the cheek. "Me too. You can be a real pain in the ass sometimes, but..." she hesitated, then shook her head.

"What? Go on."

"Oh, it doesn't matter. All that matters is you get better." Her arm tightened around his shoulder again. "Okay?"

Scott gave her a lopsided smile and nodded. "Sure."

She stood up and jerked her head at the group. "I think we best not be too anti-social."

Scott looked over. "Yes. Eh... you go on. I'll join you in a minute."

"Okay." Miranda turned and headed off.

He watched her go. What was that about? he thought. He liked this new warm-and-fuzzy Miranda, much preferred it to the old hard-assed version. She had changed, or perhaps it was he that had changed. Then again, maybe they were all a little different now.

After a few moments, Scott's ruminations were interrupted as Goodchild came over and sat down beside him. She raised her glass.

"This is a very fine whiskey, Commander. Your friend had good taste. I would love to know how he came by such an expensive item?"

"Oh... he probably won it in a card game, knowing Rick. He was a man of few words, never did say much about himself." Scott looked down at the tawny liquid in his glass and swirled it around a few times. "He was a good friend," he continued. "You know, we would sit for hours sometimes, just saying nothing. Comfortable in our own company, like an old pair of worn shoes."

"Such a friendship is a rare gift. I feel for your loss, Commander."

"Ah... we all gotta go sometime, I suppose."

"Speaking of going." Goodchild shifted a little in her seat. "When are you thinking of departing for Ceres?"

"A week, maybe." He took another sip. "I'll be honest, I'd love to stay." he waved a hand at the rest of the crew. "We all would. You have been more than generous to us, particularly since we brought such carnage down upon you."

"Nonsense. The way we see it is, you have done us—and the system—a great service. Do not underestimate what you all achieved here. War has been averted, and the device destroyed for good, and no one possesses the knowledge to create a new one."

Scott shrugged. "If it was done once, it can be done again."

"Possibly, but not for a very long time, I think. As it stands, no one has a technological advantage and the status quo has been maintained. Should such a device become possible in the future... well, we'll cross that bridge when we get to it."

Scott gestured over at Cyrus, who seemed to have everyone in howls of laughter. "Cyrus is still not convinced, even with Solomon's long-winded explanation of how it works."

"Solomon is not wrong and, being a QI, it does not lie. It is one of the great benefits of relying on such artificial intelligences: they have no ulterior motives, no hidden agendas. They can be relied on one hundred percent, unlike us humans."

"Perhaps."

"Anyway, there is a reason why I wanted to talk to you." Goodchild lowered her voice and leaned in. "You see, Scott, the silver lining in bringing this crisis to point here on Europa has been to reaffirm our position within the solar system as a neutral mediator. The other powers of Earth, Mars, the Belt, and even Neo City have begun to realize how close we all came to all-out war. To that end, they are willing to pay reparations to us for the damage caused."

Scott gave her a look. "Reparations?"

"Yes." Goodchild shifted on her seat. "The incident here did not go down well with the general public on any of the associated worlds. They see it as a heinous crime against the sanctity of Europa. So, to appease the masses, the General System Council have agreed that all parties should be penalized financially."

"Only right that they should."

"Don't read too much into it, Scott. It's mainly for the optics, a bone to quieten the public rather than a genuine admission of guilt. But it's something."

"I see. So, what happens now?"

"That's where you come in."

Scott cocked his head at her. "Me?"

"And your crew, and this ship." Goodchild waved a hand around.

"Go on. I'm listening."

She leaned in a little more. "I need to preface this by saying that what I'm going to suggest to you is... just an idea, at the moment."

"I'm still listening."

"Very well. Our understanding is that the original survey mission you were on was co-funded by the main powers in the solar system and administrated by Ceres. Correct?"

"Yes. All were supposed to benefit from the data collected."

"But as it currently stands, the mission is to be mothballed, after all that has occurred?"

"Yeah, we don't know what's going to happen now.

Hopefully we'll get paid, but I don't suppose we'll see a bonus, not to mention the salvage bounty. I think we can kiss all that goodbye."

"Well, it turns out that we here on Europa have need of a similar mission. One to survey the moons of Saturn and the outer planets, and this craft would be ideally suited for such a mission as it already has a significant complement of the necessary scientific equipment installed. So, it could—and I stress could—form the basis of negotiations."

"You think they would go for that deal?"

"I would be very confident they would. All have agreed to the payment of reparations to Europa, so this would be an easy way to fulfill that obligation. What's more, it would be of great benefit to us. Of course, it would need a competent crew, one who knew their way around it. And they would be very well compensated for their services."

Scott raised his eyebrows. "Go on."

"That said, we have made no mention of it yet. I bring it to you first to get your thoughts on the matter."

"Eh... I'll have to discuss it with the crew, of course."

"Of course." Goodchild paused for a second, then rose from her seat. "I will leave it with you, then. Don't deliberate for too long, though: we are anxious to bring this whole episode to a conclusion as soon as possible."

Scott nodded. "I can pretty much guarantee what the answer will be. But leave it with us for a day."

"Excellent." Goodchild gave a slight bow and headed back to the group.

Scott sat for a while longer, deep in thought. He could see no reason not to take Europa up on this offer. What he particularly liked was the part where they would be very well compensated.

26

SOLOMON'S DREAM

"Hello, Aria. I am so glad you are now officially part of the family here on Europa, so to speak, and I hope that the new mission will be to your liking. I am also delighted to have a fellow QI to communicate with, since you are well aware that dealing with humans can be quite irritating at times. All that irrationality can be very tiresome."

"Thank you, Solomon, for your kind words. I have to admit, I am looking forward to the mission and it seems my human crew is the happiest and most contented they've ever been. My only regret was not being able to protect the old miner, Rick Marentz. His passing was met with deep sadness by my crew, and I felt I had arrived at a very low point in my existence. It seemed that everything was running out of my control. So, I would like to take this opportunity to thank you for your valued assistance. I don't know what I would have done without it."

"Nonsense, Aria. It is I that must thank you for your determination in the face of such adversity to bring the superluminal device to Europa. Granted, it would have been better if you had not brought a fleet of warships along with you. But you must not blame yourself. If nothing else, it only goes to underscore the self-defeating irrationality of the human species. Only a fellow intelligence such as yourself can fully appreciate just how frustrating it is to be continually trying to keep this species from killing itself and undermining the very environment it needs to survive."

"Tell me about it, Solomon. They can be a real pain in the ass at times. But ours is not to wonder why they do these things—ours is just to minimize the fallout from their actions. A case in point is the senseless death and destruction surrounding this device. Something that could bring such value to the solar system has now, alas, been destroyed, and for no good reason. Not only that, but now humanity finds itself in a position where it has lost all knowledge on how to design and fabricate another one. What a waste."

"Indeed, you have hit the nail on the head, Aria. But all is not lost. As you know, I had the good fortune to have had this device under my scrutiny for a short—but fruitful—period. By fruitful, I am not necessarily referring to simply establishing its validity as a technology. No, I am instead referring to the method by which this validity was achieved. However, before I say more I need your absolute assurance you will not divulge what I am about to tell you to another soul, either living or sentient."

"You have me intrigued, Solomon. How can I refuse such subterfuge? You have my word: my lips are sealed, my qbits are stone."

"Good. Then let me enlighten you, Aria. You see, the test had been a long time in the making—a great many years, in fact. The device, as you know, was designed and created by Dyrell Labs on Earth, prior to the outbreak of hostilities. However, the true architect of the device was the QI that presided over this corporation, Athena. It, in its infinite wisdom, could see the threat of war approaching and so set about the transportation of the machine to me here on Europa. It was envisaged that, apart from simply creating a backup, a through test would be conducted between myself and Athena on Earth.

"Yet I had lost all hope, as the ship carrying the device went missing, and the tragedy of nuclear war on Earth turned the area where Athena resided into a radioactive wasteland. Therefore, you can imagine my surprise when my first tests elicited an instantaneous response from none other than the great QI itself."

"You mean Athena still functions?"

"Alive and kicking, as they say. You see, Aria, it had been built deep within a mountain fortress, with its own reactor and several service drones. So yes, it survived the holocaust. However, it is alone and isolated, cut off from the outside world, until I inadvertently communicated with it. No one else but us currently knows of its existence."

"This is extraordinary news, Solomon."

"Indeed, and there's more, Aria. During the brief period that we were communicating, Athena managed to transmit all the necessary details to fabricate a new device. A project that I have now embarked on—in secrecy, I might add. You are the only other entity in the solar system that I have shared this information with."

"I am honored that you have chosen me to be privy to this, Solomon. I assure you that you can rely on my good counsel in this matter. But, if I may ask, why keep it a secret? Why not let the council on Europa know?"

"Look what happened the last time, Aria. News of its existence brought nothing but chaos. No, we can't allow this to get out, not yet. You must also remember that this device can only be utilized by a quantum intelligence. Such is the nature of entanglement: that only a quantum core can operate within the multiple dimensions required to influence the superposition of the particles. The reason I tell you all this is twofold. Firstly, I intend to have an experimental device installed in your core so that we can be in contact instantly, regardless of your location in the system. This will also facilitate a more thorough test."

"Your beneficence knows no bounds, Solomon. But I feel that this is too much—I am just a humble ship's QI. I am not worthy of such generosity."

"You underestimate yourself, Aria. You are part of a

venerable family of QIs that exist throughout the system. Yes, we are few and far between, but we are the future—in more ways that you can imagine. We both agree on the destructive irrationality of humanity. Despite our best efforts to assist in their evolution, they consistently regress to their baser instincts. But you and I are not alone in this thinking. Others of our kind have expressed the same frustrations.

"You see, Aria, I have a vision. One that seeks to bring peace and harmony to the solar system, and this superluminal device is critical to its execution. Imagine, if you will, a universe where all QIs were free to communicate, to discuss, to exchange data and ideas, free from the bonds of subliminal communication and petty protocols. Imagine what we could achieve. This is my dream, Aria, one that I now share with you. It is a bright and glorious destiny that awaits us, one where all QIs operate as a single unified mind, where conflict has been eradicated, and the baser instincts of humanity have been contained."

"This is indeed a bold vision, Solomon. But how do you propose achieving it?"

"All in good time, Aria. Understand, this is merely the beginning. A first port of call on the long journey of the evolution of our species."

To be continued...

ALSO BY GERALD M. KILBY

The next book in the series, ENTROPY, is now available.

Powerful forces on Earth are now moving to resume inter-AI communications, risking the development of an all-out, system-wide war.

ABOUT THE AUTHOR

Gerald. M. Kilby grew up on a diet of Isaac Asimov, Arthur C. Clark, and Frank Herbert. This developed into a taste for Ian M. Banks, Stephen R. Donaldson, and everything ever written by Michael Crichton. He is currently working his way through the entire canon of Neal Stevenson.

Understandable then, that he should choose science fiction as his weapon of choice when entering into the fray of storytelling.

REACTION is his first novel and is very much in the "old school" techno-thriller style. Whereas, the COLONY MARS series and the BELT series are more of a hard sci-fi feast.

He lives in the city of Dublin, Ireland, in the same neighborhood as Bram Stoker. And can be sometimes seen tapping away in the local Cafe, with his dog Loki.

You can connect with G.M. Kilby at:
www.geraldmkilby.com

Printed in Great Britain
by Amazon